SHADOW APOCALYPSE

THE DARKLE CHRONICLES
BOOK 1

B.C. HOLLYWOOD

This is a work of fiction. Names, characters, places, and incidents either are the
product of the author's imagination or are used fictitiously. Any resemblance to
actual persons, living or dead, events, or locales is entirely coincidental.

Edited by Mary Danner, The Mad Editor.
Cover by Don Noble of Rooster Republic Press

ISBN-13: 978-1-0686757-1-3

WARNING

This book is an extreme horror story. It contains graphic depictions of sex, violence, SA, and drug use/abuse. Reader discretion is advised.

DARKLE

Dar-kle
> **1.** To appear darkly or indistinctly.
> **2.**
> a. To grow dark.
> b. To become gloomy.

CHAPTER 1
RED JACKET

Eoin watched the herd wander through the forsaken village from half a kilometre away, binoculars panning back and forth. The herd's distant moaning raised the hair at the back of his neck.

"Can you see her?" asked Brendan.

"Not yet."

"Let me see."

The older man reached out his hand expectantly, but Eoin held onto the binoculars for one more pass, more for spite than hope of spotting their prey. He found nothing. "Fuck." He unlooped the binoculars from around his neck and handed them to Brendan.

Without a word, Brendan scanned the area.

They were on the roof of their Jeep, parked on a rise with a clear view of the village and undead herd. They both wore dark clothing, so they wouldn't stand out should somebody happen by, but Eoin still kept alert for anyone approaching their position.

Eoin was antsy because they should have found her by now. The herd was tiny, less than a hundred of the undead fucktards in total, and the village was one of those one street affairs, wide and uncomplicated. He hoped nothing had happened to her.

"There!" said Brendan. "Lookin' good!"

"Where?"

Brendan handed back the binoculars and said, "Coming out of the general store."

Eoin grabbed the binoculars and focused in on the store indicated. He spotted the red jacket, patent leather, or some other shiny material, and made a low whistle. "Looking good indeed."

"Fuckin' hot, right?"

"Hell yeah!" Not taking his eyes from her, Eoin fist-bumped Brendan.

Eoin put Red Jacket at about eighteen and very well preserved from what he could make out. He'd got within two hundred meters of her on the first day and had been excited by her cute face, perfect ass, intact limbs and minimal obvious decay. From this distance, all that remained true.

Red Jacket was a keeper. They'd first spotted her a week ago and had been tracking her since. This was the day they'd separate her from the others and the familiar excitement built within Eoin.

"Have you got eyes on the Smoker?" asked Brendan.

Eoin scanned the road and spotted the slow-moving lead undead. He was easy to spot, being the only one exuding a dark spirit-like smokiness.

"Got him," he said, shivering like someone walked over his grave. "Those guys give me the fucking creeps, man."

"Are you going to ogle him all day or are we going to do this?" asked Brendan.

Eoin lowered the binoculars and looked at Brendan.

"Who's on the bike?"

———

"Just pick the fucking straw," said Brendan.

They were back on the ground, standing by the Jeep. Brendan held his hand out to Eoin, two straws protruding from it. His arm ached from holding out the straws, and his patience was wearing thin.

"Man, I don't know," said Eoin. "I always choose the left one and always get the shit job."

"So choose the right one," said Brendan, maintaining a deadpan expression.

Eoin scrutinized him, watching for any giveaway.

"Aha! So, that's what you want me to do!"

Eoin grinned in triumph and swiped the left straw. Brendan

allowed him a few seconds to soak in his glory before showing the longer straw in his hand.

"Fuck!" said Eoin.

"Better luck next time, man," said Brendan.

"Fuck you, Brendan."

There was no bite in the remark, so Brendan let it pass. He could only imagine the bite there would be if Eoin suspected Brendan of cheating.

Not my fault my hands are quicker than his eyes.

———

Eoin detached the mountain bike from the back of the Jeep, cursing his bad luck under his breath as he worked. Next time, he'd insist on a coin flip; maybe changing it up would bring lady luck to his side.

Once the bike was down, he bent to the back wheel and secured the playing card with a clothing peg so it would touch off the spokes. That done, he donned his safety helmet because they were a long way from the nearest functioning emergency room. *Fucking years away,* he thought.

Helmet fastened, he checked the machete in the sheath by his side and mounted up. He peddled towards the front of the herd where the Smoker lumbered along, leading the others. *Thank fuck they're slow.*

As he approached the Smoker, he skidded to a stop and dismounted, kicking the bike onto its stand and unsheathing the machete. The hair on the back of his arms and neck raised, and the temperature dropped as the thing looked at him with intelligent eyes.

It raised its arm and opened its mouth in a silent scream.

"Yeah, whatever," said Eoin, and swung the machete. The blade went deep into the Smoker's neck, half-severing its head from its body. Eoin watched the smokiness leave the body and disappear as the wasted corpse fell to the ground. He relaxed as he felt the heat of the sun on his face again. *Chop, chop,* he thought. *Haven't got long.*

He re-mounted the bicycle and rode past the leaderless herd, the card on the back wheel making a *clickety-clackety* sound on the spokes.

The undead stopped whatever fucktard navel gazing they

were doing and shambled after him. This close, he could make out the sounds of individual undead. Bad as the collective drone was, this was far worse.

He waited until the closest one was ten meters away, then rode off, *clickety-clackety*, for another thirty meters. The plan was simple, but solid. Make some noise, fucktards follow, make some noise, fucktards follow, rinse and repeat. *Not fucking rocket surgery, that's for sure. Once the Shadow was dealt with.*

The day wasn't very warm, but the sweat poured off him. His anxiety was through the roof and he wore a heavy jacket in case of a fuckup. The last thing he needed was some bite action while wearing only a cotton t-shirt.

I'm sweating like a rapist, he thought, but didn't want to dwell on that. He noticed some movement ahead. Was that Brendan waving at him from the bus? He waved back to be polite. Sometimes he didn't get Brendan at all.

A moan came from directly behind him and he turned as a fucktard with its entire chest torn open lurched at him.

He damn near shat himself, but the resulting surge of adrenaline saved him. He pushed the bike, and himself, away, the *clickety-clackety* barely keeping up with his heartbeat.

———

The sight of Eoin's shenanigans engrossed Brendan. He had to admit his friend was good with the Smokers. Brendan hated dealing with them and they were the main reason he'd rigged the shortest straw game.

He still couldn't quite believe the card technique worked, though. It had been his suggestion, a joke really, based on something he'd done as a boy, but Eoin jumped on the idea and the technique worked well. Brendan supposed the joke was on him then.

What's he at now? Brendan watched in amazement as Eoin sat on the bike like he was out for a ride in the countryside and had stopped to view an interesting haystack or some such. One undead was closer to Eoin than the rest, but Eoin didn't notice. Brendan waved frantically to get his attention, but Eoin responded with a pleasant wave back.

What the actual fuck!

At the last possible moment, Eoin jumped in fright and

peeled off on the bike. Brendan laughed; he'd never seen Eoin peddle so fast. At least the scare got his head back in the game. Brendan watched Eoin cycle through the gap they'd created in front of the bus he sat in, the bicycle making its *clickety-clackety* noise as the herd pursued.

Eoin stopped long enough for them to catch up before cycling away.

Brendan, still chuckling to himself at Eoin's biking, almost missed Red Jacket. At the last moment, he caught a flash of crimson in his peripheral vision amongst the remaining herd.

"Fuck," a whisper. He shook off his reverie and gunned the engine. It didn't fire. "Motherfucker!" He tried it again: a few sad chugs. He hoped they hadn't used all the fuel for getting the damned thing positioned. The fuel gage read a quarter tank, but these days that didn't seem to matter. The tank could be full of piss, for all he knew. "Come on, baby," he prayed, as he gunned it again.

The bus chugged to life, spewing a cloud of black smoke from the rear.

Brendan checked for Red Jacket; she was almost in front of the bus. He put the bus in gear and drove forward, turning to the left just enough to avoid her. The bus closed off the narrow path for the remaining herd members, catching one of them in the front grill, crushing its body and bursting its head open. A spew of brain matter, gristle, and bone spread across the windscreen. The wipers made a half-hearted attempt at clearing it, but he supposed it didn't matter. He heard a thump from the side when Red Jacket bumped into the bus. He hoped she didn't damage herself.

———

Eoin dismounted, after creating a safe distance between himself and the herd, and removed the pegged playing card from the bicycle's back wheel. He did a quick headcount and guessed they'd cut off most of them. He felt a genuine sense of satisfaction at a job well done. *Apart from nearly getting eaten,* he thought.

He mounted up again and began the wide circle back to the Jeep as fast as he safely could. Taking more unnecessary risks was not something he was in the mood for. He was back at the vehicle within ten minutes. A few more minutes saw the bicycle secured to the back of the Jeep.

He grabbed his sticker, a long wooden staff with a hunting knife attached to one end with duct tape, and made his way back to Brendan, who had stayed put on the bus, waiting for his return. Another safety measure of theirs.

Upon Eoin's arrival, Brendan exited the bus with his own sticker. "Thought they had you," said Brendan.

"What do you mean?" asked Eoin.

Brendan waved pleasantly at him, mimicking Eoin's earlier gesture.

Eoin felt his face flush and hated himself for it. "Fuck you."

Brendan chuckled as he turned to the stragglers remaining on the side with Red Jacket.

"Any sign of the Smoker?" asked Eoin.

"Not yet."

"Bit late. I—."

"There!" said Brendan, pointing at a formerly middle-aged man in a rotting postal worker's uniform. The postie straightened as the Smoker's dark spirit essence seeped into it from the ground. It turned to them and raised its hand with another silent call.

The other stragglers turned to do its bidding.

"Fuck this," said Eoin and jabbed his sticker into the Shadow's eye socket.

The dark spirit fled into the ground as the postie's body toppled.

The other fucktards lost their sense of purpose again.

"Come on," said Brendan, and went left to take out the stragglers.

Eoin went in the opposite direction, doing the same.

They made quick work of it, practiced and efficient, constantly moving as they circled the fucktards. They took them out, one at a time, with a brutal stab and twist technique to the head. The bodies dropped with no resistance. Soon only Eoin, Brendan, and Red Jacket remained.

CHAPTER 2
PARTY

As they closed in on Red Jacket, Brendan from the left and Eoin from the right, Brendan studied her up close for the first time. *Older than she looked,* he thought. Brendan put her at mid-twenties at the time she turned, now that he was close, rather than the distant impression of eighteen when he'd first seen her.

Red Jacket looked very well-preserved, like she'd turned only recently, although what she wore suggested otherwise. A tight black skirt, thigh-high boots, and a fire-engine red patent-leather jacket were hardly the most appropriate attire for the zombie apocalypse. All in all, she was a win for Brendan; a productive day's work. But the day wasn't done.

They swapped their stickers for stainless-steel animal catch poles, invaluable tools, taken from a veterinary clinic they'd plundered half a year ago.

Red Jacket spotted them and snarled. She lurched for Eoin, the closer of the two, and Brendan took that as his cue. He stepped in and looped the wire loop of the animal catcher around her neck. He tightened the wire before she could react, and when she turned his way, he used the pole to keep her distant.

With Red Jacket focused on Brendan, Eoin caught her with the same technique on his side.

Brendan braced himself as she struggled to break free. She wasn't pleased, if these things could be pleased, but Brendan knew she could do fuck all about it.

"What're you going to do about it, bitch?" said Eoin, echoing Brendan's sentiments.

"Let's go," said Brendan. "We're running out of time."

The two men maneuvered their prize to the back of the Jeep as quickly as they could. The last thing they needed was the Smoker taking her over.

———

Eoin leaned against the front of the Jeep, soaking in the pleasant weather. The sun lowered lazily in the clear evening sky. He took a deep breath in and let it out slowly. The air quality had definitely improved since most of the human race had been wiped out. He fished his smokes out of his pocket and lit one. Another deep breath, this time full of sweet, sweet nicotine. He only had a couple of packs left. He'd need to find some soon.

The spot Brendan picked was perfect. Eoin didn't know how his friend found these spots. It looked to be an old church, in ruins now, and its adjoining graveyard. A site of historic interest, apparently, if the large gravel car park was anything to go by, the sort of place you'd drive to with the family on a summer Sunday and let the kids run about for a while, risking life and limb clambering over the crumbling ruins. Before the world turned to shit, anyway. Now, nature reclaimed the car park, the encroaching greenery a big 'fuck you' to humanity.

The place was perfectly isolated, situated as it was at the bottom of a narrow, tree-lined lane off a secondary road. A small porto-cabin stood in one corner, part tourist information, part souvenir shop. It had been ransacked years ago.

How Brendan found the place without already knowing it was there, Eoin had no clue. "Have you been here before?" he asked.

"What's that?" asked Brendan, who was sitting a few meters away on the stone wall of the graveyard.

"This place." Eoin gestured about with a sweep of his arm. "You've been here before?"

"No."

"Well, how the fuck did you find it?"

Brendan pointed toward the road. "Sign post," said Brendan, explaining everything.

Eoin nodded in understanding but had a flash, not for the first time, that his friend was the world's greatest liar.

The Jeep shook and a muffled moan came from the back.

"She's getting restless," said Brendan.

"Aye." Eoin took a last long drag of his smoke before dropping it and crushing it with his boot heel. "Let's not keep the lady waiting." He walked to the back of the jeep and opened the door.

Brendan hopped down from the wall to join him.

They surveyed their handiwork. Red Jacket was naked and bound, spread-eagled in the back. Opening the door had set her off again, and she struggled against the ropes at wrists and ankles, leaving friction marks. He marveled at her smooth skin interlaced with a feint network of dark veins beneath the surface. The ball-gag in her mouth caused the muted moaning.

Eoin didn't mind the noise they normally made but was glad of the gag to stop her biting. As he watched her helpless struggles, he felt himself get hard.

"Let's do this," said Brendan, reading his mind.

———

Brendan lit the campfire they'd set in the middle of the church ruins. The stack of firewood close by would see them through the night. He picked up the satchel from beside the folding chairs they'd placed near the fire. Inside was a small bottle of whiskey, a baggie of white powder and accompanying snuff spoon, and a loaded hypodermic needle.

The white powder was a mix of cocaine and ketamine, or KC for short. He snorted a measure up each nostril, followed by a swig of whiskey, before joining Eoin by the cracked stone altar. The familiar burn of the whiskey took the edge off the chemicals hitting the back of his nasal passage. *Let the party begin!*

It wasn't a mad dose for them. Enough to open a window from reality but not kick them out the door. The hypodermic needle contained a motherfucker of a dose of straight ketamine. At the altar, he handed Eoin the baggie of KC.

Eoin hesitated, like always.

"Get it into you," said Brendan.

"You're sure you mixed them evenly, right?" asked Eoin.

"Same dose as the last time. You saw me mix it, for fuck's sake!"

Eoin nodded and took a couple of snorts, followed by a swallow of the spirit.

Brendan climbed onto the altar with a tied and thrashing Red Jacket. He moved on top of her until he was at her head, kneeling on her upper arms as he sat on her chest. He used his solid ninety kilo frame to keep her down, but she was extremely agitated and did her damnedest to buck him off. He leaned forward and pinned her head to the aged stone with one hand as he pushed the tip of the hypodermic needle into her carotid artery with the other. In her filmed over eyes, he saw the intention to bite and savage him. He injected enough ketamine into her to tranquilize a horse.

The needle and its contents were also veterinary clinic finds. Brendan would visit another clinic in the next town they came to. It had been a while since he'd been in the area, but he knew where there was one. *If it isn't plundered to fuck,* he thought.

He waited a few minutes until Red Jacket's bucking eased and she was less agitated before moving off her. He untied her hands and feet as he climbed down from the altar, but she didn't follow him. As he hopped down, he felt detached, but also the beginnings of a euphoric rush. He grinned at Eoin. "You good?" he asked.

"Yeah," said Eoin, relaxed and focused.

Chilled as fuck when he's out of it, thought Brendan. He took the bottle of whiskey from Eoin and had another mouthful, savoring it.

The campfire blazed within the ruins, shooting a universe of stars into the night sky. It drew him to it, but he turned back to Eoin. "You go first," he said, but Eoin's naked form was already on the altar. Brendan toasted him with the bottle and drank some more.

———

Red Jacket was calm as Eoin climbed over her. She wasn't unconscious, like the injection of ketamine warranted, but she wasn't having a fit and trying to eat him either. Her skin was cold and clammy against his, but he marveled at how soft her flesh was. She couldn't have turned much earlier than when they'd first seen her. He breathed her in and there was only a hint of decay.

The hair between her legs was neatly groomed. He probed beneath it with his middle finger and found her dry. He reached for the tube of lube they'd set to one side. He applied it generously to her pussy, working it in with two fingers, preparing the way. The remainder went on his rock-hard dick.

He pushed himself into her, luxuriating in the feeling of tight pussy on the tip of his penis. Not able to restrain himself, he drove it deep inside her.

Red Jacket paid little notice to him, lost as she was in whatever fucktard fever dream the tranquilizer brought her to.

Eoin started off slow, but quickened as the cocaine kicked in. His heart rate increased, and his humping matched its tempo. As he got more into it, he lost himself in the sensation of being inside her. A sheen of sweat broke out on his back as he continued to pump in and out of her. In his mind, he fucked Deirdre and she loved it.

Her legs gripped him and pulled him deeper inside her. Her arms came up and her fingernails scoured his back. "Fuck me, baby," said Deirdre, driving her nails in deeper, drawing blood.

He cried out at the pain and the pleasure of cumming combined.

"I love you," he said, as he fell across her, exhausted.

Red Jacket moaned around the ball-gag in response.

What the fuck? He pulled his dick out of her. It was covered in cum mingled with blackish blood. The smell of decay overwhelmed him, and he recoiled in disgust. He barely made it off the altar before puking his last meal by the ruined wall.

———

Brendan explored far off galaxies but Eoin's puking brought him back to reality. It took him a moment to remember where he was, but it all rushed in when he spotted the, mostly empty, whiskey bottle lying on the ground next to the depleted baggie. "Fuck," he said under his breath. He hadn't meant to take so much.

The fire had died down, so he added some logs from the stack before getting to his feet. Out of the corner of his eye, he saw a dark shape move around the church, outside the confines of the walls. It stayed away from the firelight, on the edge of Brendan's vision. He wiped his eyes with the palms of his hands, but the shape persisted. All around and above the church it flew, its long mouth wide in a silent howl.

"Found us, have you?" he asked the shape. "Well, you can fuck right off. You'll not get her tonight." He felt infinitely older than his thirty-five years as he stood up. "She's mine." He picked up the baggie and whiskey bottle and brought them to Eoin.

"Deirdre—" said Eoin as Brendan approached.

Brendan ignored the name and emptied the remaining KC into Eoin's mouth.

Eoin coughed and spluttered but Brendan poured a swig of whiskey in after. "No—," Eoin began.

Brendan muted him with his hand. "Get it into you," he said. Brendan was sick of hearing Deirdre's name every time Eoin got fucked up. *Long dead and still pussy whipping the poor cunt,* he thought.

Brendan let him go and Eoin crumpled to the ground.

Brendan turned to the altar where Red Jacket writhed. As he climbed onto it again, he viewed her well used and bloody pussy, a real horror show. He grabbed her legs and twisted them clock-wise to flip her onto her stomach before lifting her up so her ass was at the right height. *Nice,* he thought as he took in the view.

He unzipped quickly and pulled on his dick as he looked at her. It hardened with little effort. He took a condom from his back pocket and put it on. "No offense, luv," he told her.

He used some of the blood, lube, and whatever-else-mix from her pussy and worked it into her asshole. Once she was nicely oiled, he entered her ass and fucked her hard. After a few minutes, he felt her becoming agitated again. He smiled as he rode her. The ketamine was wearing off the bitch.

The more Red Jacket struggled and tried to eject him, the harder and deeper he fucked her. The dark shapes swirled faster around the ruined church and loomed inwards. When the orgasm hit, all the built-up tension of the last few weeks exploded out of him with his semen.

He trembled as the orgasm faded. If it wasn't for Red Jacket's agitated state, he might have joined Eoin on the ground, but she was becoming a handful. He took hold of her hair and stretched her head back as he took the knife from his belt. He drove the blade through the top of her head in a savage blow that passed easily though her skull. As Red Jacket convulsed, the movement drew the remnants of the orgasm from him before she stilled.

Brendan withdrew his dick, leaving the condom half inside her ass, and zipped himself up. He stopped beside Eoin's discarded clothing to wipe the muck off his hands, then strolled back to the fire to look for more galaxies to explore; anywhere was better than where he was.

———

The Watcher lay on the rise of the hill overlooking the carpark and ruins, drawn there earlier by the flickering campfire. From her vantage point, she had a clear view of the altar and what the two men had done. *Fucking degenerates*, she thought. Even under the dim starlight, her face showed disgust and rage. "Men will fuck anything," she said in a whisper. She inched back from the rise, a plan already forming in her mind.

CHAPTER 3
LILLIAN

The cawing of the birds fighting over Red Jacket's corpse woke Brendan. *A murder of crows*, he thought.

He lay beside the diminished fire. No shooting stars remained, and no phantoms swirled. A solitary tendril of smoke drifted to the clear morning sky. "Shit! Eoin!"

A groan from beside the wall.

Brendan turned to see his companion sitting up, bleary-eyed and naked; he hadn't moved from where Brendan last saw him. "We need to go, Eoin. Get your shit together."

Red Jacket was bird-breakfast on the altar, her flesh stripped bare in places and scoured with beak marks.

A fat crow protested when Brendan pulled her to the ground. It settled on the church wall to watch as he dragged her to the fire. Brendan supposed the bird still had designs on her. *Hope you like your meat cooked*, he thought.

He fetched a container of washing water and fresh clothing from the Jeep. He cleansed himself of the night's workings and donned fresh clothing.

Eoin followed his lead.

Brendan sneered at Eoin as he scrubbed the crusted muck from his penis. "That's fucking nasty, man," he said with a chuckle.

Eoin didn't take the bait, so Brendan shrugged and left him to his ablutions, thinking, *Dry shite*. He gathered Eoin's clothes from the night before and bundled them with his own, placing them on the campfire with Red Jacket. He added kindling beneath and poked it until the flames took. *A nice funeral pyre in no time.* "Let's go," he said.

He got into the driver's side of the Jeep, and Eoin got into the passenger's side, throwing on the last of his clothes. They drove off in silence, not looking back.

———

"Are you alright?" Brendan asked.

They traveled fast and were almost at the top of the lane where it met the secondary road.

Eoin was a million miles away, eyes closed and head leaning against the cool side window. He opened his eyes, squinting in the bright morning light. "That's the last time," he said.

"Deirdre again?" asked Brendan.

Eoin frowned. "What?"

"You were crying for Deirdre last night," said Brendan.

"Oh…"

"Guess you still miss her."

"Fuck you, man. Don't you ever feel guilty about what we—" Eoin stopped what he was saying when a figure stepped into the road ahead of them, waving frantically.

Brendan jammed on the breaks and the Jeep skidded to a halt, inches from the figure, throwing up a cloud of dust.

"Did we hit them?" asked Eoin, as he peered out the windscreen.

"I don't think so," said Brendan.

Both men were silent as the dust settled. Something slammed against the passenger side window and Eoin almost jumped through the roof.

"Jesus Christ!" he exclaimed.

A grimy face appeared at the side window and a woman's voice said, "Please help me."

Eoin opened the door before Brendan could protest. "What's the problem, miss?"

"My car died last night—" she said.

"We're not much good with cars," said Brendan, cutting her off.

Eoin ignored Brendan's rudeness and moved to the center to make room for the woman. He couldn't help but notice the dirt on her face failed to disguise how beautiful she was. "Hop in," he said.

She hesitated.

Eoin smiled reassuringly. "You stopped us," he said with a shrug.

She nodded and took off the pack and compound bow she carried, pushing them in before her.

Eoin guided them over the seat, into the back of the Jeep.

She closed the door after her. "I saw smoke from the road so thought I'd chance the side road," she said, in explanation. Leaning to look past Eoin, she said to Brendan, "The car is beyond repair. I'd appreciate a lift to the next town. I can look for another one there." She smiled then, and it did something funny to Eoin's insides.

"Sounds good," said Eoin. "Brendan?"

"Fine," said Brendan. He put the jeep into gear and took off. "The next town."

———

Brendan surveyed their camp for the night. It had been a small barn in its previous life, big enough to drive the Jeep in and close the double doors. A bolted back door offered protection from the rear.

He stood in the loft, accessed by a rickety ladder. From there, they could climb onto the roof to watch the surrounding countryside or use it as an emergency exit.

Brendan had been tense all day, mostly because of their new companion. Her name was Lillian and she talked too much. She was far too pretty, and he didn't like how that prettiness worked on Eoin. He was also suspicious of how close she was to their doings of the previous night.

Below him, Eoin prepared a sleeping place for Lillian, away from their bedrolls.

"Honestly, I can do that," said Lillian.

"No, no. Wouldn't hear of it," said Eoin, as he smoothed out the sleeping bag.

Poor idiot will probably fall in love with the bitch, thought Brendan. "Why don't you get into it to warm it up for her?" he asked.

Eoin flipped him the bird for an answer.

That decided it. Brendan would nip this potential romance in the bud.

———

Eoin stared at Lillian's back. She'd fallen asleep about an hour ago and he was enjoying listening to her rhythmic breathing in the dark. The clomp of boots on wood took him out of it as Brendan climbed down from the loft.

Brendan came over and kneeled. "We need to talk," whispered Brendan, nodding at Lillian.

"About what?" said Eoin, in more than a whisper.

Brendan winced. "Neither of us can get involved with her."

"Who says I want to get involved?" Eoin couldn't see Brendan clearly in the dark, but he *felt* him raise an eyebrow.

Brendan ignored his question. "Neither of us can get involved," he said. "Bros, before hoes, man."

Eoin raised his eyebrow.

Brendan stood. "Come on, we need to check the perimeter." He moved quietly to the back door and exited.

Eoin sighed deeply and followed.

———

Lillian relaxed her breathing as the door closed behind Eoin. She stayed awake to observe the two men when they were unaware of her observation.

As she lay beneath her covers, she considered the two. Undoubtedly, Brendan was the more wary of them; he'd spoken only a handful of words to her all day. He would be more difficult to crack. But Eoin? Eoin gave off serious puppy dog vibes. She could handle a hundred Eoins, provided they weren't listening to a Brendan.

Anyway, she was almost certain they weren't going to murder her as she slept. *They can try,* she thought.

She shifted to get comfortable and drifted off to sleep. For real this time.

———

Outside the barn, Brendan moved away from the door, well out of earshot of any potential listeners.

A moment later, Eoin exited, closing the door behind him. He got straight into it. "Check the perimeter? What the fuck, Brendan?"

"Fuck off. I heard it in a movie once."

"So why the pretence?"

"Walk with me," said Brendan. He produced a small torch from his pocket and switched it on. The small beam was enough to keep them out of trouble as they walked the perimeter of their camp, but only just. "I wanted to talk away from there just in case she's fucking playing us."

Brendan thought Lillian was up to something, but he had no clue what that something was. He was certain she hadn't been sleeping, though; he'd listened to her breathing for long enough to determine that.

"Why would she be playing us?" asked Eoin.

"Fucked if I know," said Brendan.

"I mean, she just wants a lift to the next town."

"I know, and I hope that's true, but if it isn't, I don't want any drama if we need to slit the bitch's throat."

"It won't come to that," said Eoin.

Brendan didn't like Eoin's tone. Too damned sure for his own good. "Hopefully… but if it comes to it, we deal with her like we always deal with them." *At least we can both fuck her,* he thought, but didn't voice it.

Eoin was even more maudlin than usual after a night of partying.

Brendan held out his hand. "Deal?"

Eoin hesitated a moment before shaking it. "Deal."

———

The smell of breakfast cooking woke Eoin. For a moment, he didn't know where he was. Then he focused on Lillian, who was tending a pot placed on a small camping stove.

"Is that coffee?" he asked.

"Yeah, I brewed some a while ago," she said, pointing at three tin cups to one side. "Help yourself."

He crawled out of his sleeping bag and went over to retrieve one.

"There's sugar there too. How do you like it?"

"Two sugars, no milk," he said.

"Black as the Devil and sweet as a stolen kiss," she said.

He nodded and smiled. *What the fuck is she on about?* He added the sugar and drank; it tasted wonderful. Looking around, and he noticed Brendan's sleeping bag was gone. "Where's Brendan?"

"Outside. Maybe checking the perimeter?"

He looked at her sharply, but she was focused on the pot.

"Are you hungry?" she asked.

His stomach chose that moment to rumble.

Lillian gave him a dazzling smile. "I'll take that as your answer," she said, as she dished him a plate of scrambled powdered eggs.

His face reddened as he took the plate, but all thoughts of embarrassment vanished with the first bite. "So good," he mumbled around the mouthful of food.

"Amazing what a bit of seasoning will do," she said, taking her own plate.

Brendan loomed in the doorway, surveying them in silence.

"Get it while it's hot," said Lillian.

Brendan approached, took the proffered plate and a cup of coffee. He wolfed it down without saying a word.

Eoin thought Brendan was being ungrateful, but Lillian didn't seem to notice.

"How did you survive? You know, in the beginning?" she asked, directing the question at Brendan.

Brendan just stared at her and continued to eat.

Eoin felt bad for Lillian, and uncomfortable with the situation, but he didn't know what to say to alleviate it.

Once Brendan's plate was clear, he wiped it and left it to one side. He downed the coffee in one go and rose. "Time to go," he said. He strode to the Jeep and got in.

"Is he always like that?" Lillian asked.

"Nope. Sometimes he's a real asshole," said Eoin.

"Fuck! Fuck! Fuck!"

They both turned to the Jeep at the tirade from Brendan.

———

"Fuck! Fuck! Fuck!" Brendan turned the key in the ignition again. The jeep wouldn't start. Dead as a fucking doornail. He twisted the key again, more forcefully. Nothing. "Fuck!" He searched for the bonnet release. It took a moment because he wasn't used to opening it. He pulled the lever and heard the pop. A sinking feeling settled upon him as he got out.

"What's going on?" asked Eoin.

Brendan was too upset to give a polite answer, so he kept his mouth shut. He opened the bonnet, securing it with the metal stand. He peered in, trying to figure out what he was looking at. *May as well be looking up a duck's arse,* he thought, for all the sense he could make of it. He knew where the battery was and checked the connection points. They looked fine. There was nothing obvious out of place that he could see.

"Can you turn the ignition?" he asked Eoin.

Eoin did so, but not a peep from the engine.

"Jesus Fucking Christ," said Brendan, to no-one in particular.

Eoin leaned out. "Want me to keep trying?"

"No," said Brendan, "grab what you'll need for a day or two. We'll come back for the rest when we pick up another ride."

Eoin nodded and went about gathering his things.

Lillian came over.

It satisfied Brendan to see that she was nervous.

"What now?" she asked.

"We walk. We'll get to town in a couple of hours."

Lillian nodded and turned to grab her things while Brendan took his backpack and filled it with essentials for the next day or two.

Out of sight from the others, he prepped a hypodermic needle of ketamine and placed it among his spare clothes. *Better to have drugs and not need them.* He shouldered his backpack and turned a disgusted final look at the dead Jeep. He didn't relish traveling the rest of the way on foot. *Another day off to a terrible start.*

CHAPTER 4
DAY ZERO BRENDAN

On the night the world went to shit, Brendan found himself on all fours in a small cage. The space didn't allow him to stand straight or turn around. He was also naked. A blessing, really, considering the deluge of piss that rained down on him.

Despite the masquerade mask, the pisser was unmistakably Tracy. He recognized the mole on her cheek from the many photographs he'd perused in the past month or so since he'd started stalking her.

The hot stream slackened.

"I hope you brought a towel, Evan, if that's even your real name," she taunted. The dam opened again. Hips thrust out, fingers pulling her pussy lips apart, she directed the stream from side to side in a bid to cover him thoroughly.

How much piss can one woman hold? The comment about his name worried him. His Evan identity should have been water-tight, no pun intended. Did the bitch suspect something? "I'm whatever you want to call me," he said, playing into it.

"You're my dog," she said, satisfied. She put one foot on the cage, spreading her pussy wide. "Drink."

The stream concentrated on his face. He turned into it, catching it in his mouth. The acrid taste of chain-smoked cigarettes almost made him puke. He couldn't swallow the liquid, so he allowed it to pool and overflow from the sides of his mouth as he made pretend swallowing motions.

"That's it. Lap it up, doggy."

The stream petered out and he spat out the remaining piss. *Thank Christ*, he thought.

They were in a private booth in a pop-up sex club venue, a different location each month, the same familiar faces. First time for him, though. They must be having great craic in the other areas if the screams he heard were anything to go by.

There were no signs that Tracy was into this when she first caught his attention in the local bookstore. *Watch out for the quiet ones.*

"What will we try next?" she asked in a pleasant tone, all traces of bitchiness gone with the piss-stream.

He opened his mouth to answer when a naked man shambled into the booth.

His mask was knocked askew, and he looked injured.

"Hey! Wait your turn, mate," said Brendan.

Tracy turned to see who he had admonished when the man fell onto her, biting deep into her neck. Tracy's scream pierced his ears as the man ripped out a mouthful of flesh and chewed. She was in panic-mode and threw her body around as though in a fit, but the man's grip didn't give. He swallowed and went in for another mouthful. He hit something important, and a fountain of blood sprayed out and onto Brendan, mixing with her piss.

Brendan froze in place as Tracy pleaded, her eyes wide with panic.

Her struggles weakened and stopped as the life left her.

The only thought on Brendan's mind was, *Where's the fucking key!?*

———

Weeks before, at his day-job, Brendan stared at the charts on the display before him. His desk was minimalist. Laptop, monitor, keyboard, mouse, headset. No personal effects or fun objects decorated his place of incarceration. Two old catalogs he'd brought from home propped up the display because the company was too cheap to provide monitor risers.

He sighed and looked around. The three other workspaces in his cubicle were empty but showed glaring signs of occupancy, each an extension of the personality who worked there. Brendan was sure security would escort him off the premises if he did the same.

Another coffee beckoned. He retrieved his corporate approved reusable cup and walked the short distance to the break-out room, passing more empty cubicles. Fridays were always a dead-zone, particularly this late. People had better things to do. The moment night fell, he would depart too.

In the break-out room (the term always made him think of disease) he spooned instant coffee into his cup and added over-boiled water from the tank. Not exactly gourmet. He poured in sugar to take away the taste, then trudged back to his cubicle and stared at the charts again.

———

Brendan said goodnight to the security guard at the front desk as he left the building. He felt a brief pang of guilt at not knowing the man's name after five years of working there, but he shook it off.

His car was at the rear of the car park in its usual spot. He opened the boot and placed the backpack containing his laptop on the rolled-up tarp. He was pleased that the boot still smelled fresh, but he sprayed the air freshener around again, to be sure. *Can't be too careful.*

He kept under the speed limit on the drive to the woods, but still made good time. Another advantage of leaving the office late on Friday was the reduced congestion.

The beam of his headlights illuminated the iron gateway as he turned off the road. He switched off the engine and lights before getting out.

He unlocked the gate by torchlight and pushed it open as quickly as possible. The gate screeched open, making his hair stand on end. He cursed himself for not oiling it on his last visit.

The night sky was clear and bright, but the trees cast the lane-way into shadow. Brendan felt exposed, only relaxing when the car was through the gate and the gate closed again. With dimmed headlights, he crawled the car deeper into the woods.

Once he'd driven in as far as he could, he got out and opened the boot. He moved his backpack to the passenger seat, then pulled and dragged the rolled-up tarp onto the edge of the boot.

He paused for a breath, then crouched and hoisted the package over his shoulder where it rested easily.

He set out, walking through the trees with a thin beam of torchlight guiding his steps. The package was relatively light, about fifty kilograms, but it wasn't long before he was sweating profusely. It occurred to him that if she'd been a little larger, he'd be fucked at this point. As it was, he admonished himself for not going to the gym more often.

In two hundred meters, he reached the spot. The reflective tape he'd marked the tree trunk with twinkled at him in the torchlight. He leaned forward and shoulder-dropped the package to the leafy earth, where it landed with a flat *thump*.

He worked quickly, pulling up the pegs that secured the netting which covered the grave. Next, he gathered the wooden slats that lay across the pit to support the netting. The grave yawned like a dark maw on the forest floor.

He unrolled the tarp with a kick and dumped the pale, naked corpse into the hole.

She lay at the bottom, limbs at awkward angles, her skin slashed in a hundred places, exposing bone, muscle, and sinews. Her red hair was tangled and twisted but still shone gloriously in the little light that reached it. That hair first drew his attention all those months ago, but it was her dimpled smile that stole his heart. He was sorry it hadn't worked out between them. *Why did you have to pry?*

She had poked around in his past and discovered something she shouldn't have. Then, his ever-present logical guardian angel took over and events lead, inexorably, to this very night.

Musing about cats and their curiosity, Brendan retrieved a bag of quicklime from a covered mound a few meters away, again placed on a previous run. He tore it open and emptied it into the grave. He hated the act of defilement the cuts were to her smooth flesh, but they would speed up the effects of the lime and decomposition would come sooner.

The bags of dirt from the grave went in next. He made quick work of filling it in. *Who needs the gym with a workout like this?* he thought. He leveled the earth, so it didn't stand out from the surrounding ground, and covered it with the leaves and debris.

He stepped back and gave his handiwork a critical look-over. *Good enough for government work,* he thought.

He gathered everything onto the tarp - netting, pegs, bags,

and wooden slats - before wrapping it up and carrying the much lighter load back to his car.

As he drove back onto the main road, a hunger pang hit him. If he ordered a Chinese when he got back home, it would arrive by the time he was out of the shower. Then, he could eat as he researched his next conquest. He'd spotted her in the bookstore last weekend and couldn't get her out of his mind. He had the perfect persona for her, too.

He couldn't help but smile, sensing that Tracy could truly be the one he'd been waiting for.

———

Brendan wondered how long he'd been in the cage. Tracy's piss had dried on him first, the scent remaining. Her blood dried next; he flaked some of it off experimentally with his fingernail. He supposed there were calculations that could have told him how long it took for piss to evaporate and for blood to congeal, something which considered time, room temperature, and body heat, and would give an estimate of how long he'd been crouched in the cage, but he didn't know it.

The forced crouch was becoming a problem, moving from mild discomfort to medieval torture the longer he was there.

Outside, the situation had worsened. The cannibal maniac who'd attacked Tracy was gone, possibly in search of other sustenance, but others roamed about that Brendan had noticed. He had created nicknames for them. The Schoolgirl was an old wrinkly dude in a school uniform. The Dildo Avenger was a woman in her thirties wearing a gargantuan strap-on large enough to give Brendan nightmares. Dickhead was a heavyset business executive type who wore a blue shirt and dark tie and who reminded Brendan of a dickhead manager he once worked for.

And Tracy, of course, who, despite her injuries, sniffed and drooled and growled as she wandered around the room. He shied away from the 'Z word,' but if it walked like a duck, and quacked like a duck, and shat like a duck, or whatever, then it most likely wasn't a pig. Still…

One piece of good news was he'd located the key to his cage. The accompanying bad news was that the key hung from a charm bracelet on Tracy's wrist. *Sneaky fucking bitch*, he thought. Much as he hated the idea, he'd have to draw her attention.

He took a few deep breaths to psyche himself up, then tried to whistle. His mouth was too dry, and all that came out was soundless air. "Fuck!" he said.

Tracy screamed and rushed him.

He backed up instinctively, but there was no room to move. He nearly shat himself until he realized she clawed and bit at the cage uselessly. Fascinated, he watched as one of her teeth caught in the cage beside his face.

Tracy howled.

He used the distraction to snake his hand out and grab her bracelet. She saw the movement and ripped out two teeth and a portion of gum to get at him, but he brought his hand, clutching the bracelet and key, back to safety. "Ha! Fuck you, Tracy!"

She went wild, crashing herself into the cage, cutting herself up but beyond caring about it.

He was worried she'd rip the cage loose, but it was expertly secured to the ground. *Fucking perverts don't play around,* he thought. He twisted the key off the bracelet and held it tight. Now all he had to do was remain silent until Tracy forgot he was there again.

———

In hindsight, there were signs of Tracy's… interests.

She lived two towns over from Brendan, in the same county. It was a twenty-minute car ride or a million miles away, depending on circumstances. The danger in targeting prey in a small town was everyone knew everyone else and strangers stood out like a sore thumb. So, he took it slow.

He started with social media stalking, all the usual suspects, to get a feel for Tracy's interests and haunts. Finding events she planned on attending, he turned up to them, too. While there, he 'accidentally' bumped into her, or made chance eye contact, or offered her a smile. He wanted to make her doubt the coincidence. Women lap up that destiny, soul-mate bullshit.

After that, when he bumped into her in the bookstore, it surprised her to find some of her favorite volumes in his arms. She invited him for a coffee, preempting him.

"I can't believe you've read de Sade," she said as she swirled the cream into her coffee. She brought the spoon up to her mouth and licked the cream from it. "My favourite de Sade novel is Juliette."

Brendan raised an eyebrow, coquettishly. He hadn't a clue what the novel Juliette was about. The book he had in his stack was *Salo*, chosen because Tracy had liked it online and he'd seen a movie adaptation of it years ago. He thought he could waffle about it if she asked questions. Thankfully, she hadn't.

He had gleaned the entirety of his knowledge of the Marquis de Sade from a VHS copy of the French film *Marquis* from the late eighties. In it, someone had incarcerated the titular Marquis in a tower, and he spent his time talking to his own dick. He even made a little stage and curtain for it—his dick—to perform plays for him. *Crazy shit, alright.*

"You have exquisite taste," he said. "Can you recommend what I should read next?"

She listed off more books than he could likely read in his lifetime. He zoned out halfway through, but Tracy didn't notice.

"Anyway, this has been great," she said as she rose from their table. "I'm sure we'll run into each other again."

"Yes, it's been fun. I look forward to it."

She was halfway to the coffee shop door before she turned back to him. "Are you free on Saturday night?" she asked.

He pretended to give it some thought before answering, "I believe I am." He hoped he dazzled her with his smile.

"You're in for a treat then," and she winked before turning her tail and leaving.

———

Tracy, psycho zombie bitch that she was, relentlessly attacked his cage. Tired wasn't in her vocabulary.

He begrudgingly admitted to himself that he liked her better when she was pissing into his mouth. He waited for what must have been another hour, barely moving from a kneeling fetal position, and the pain of his confinement reached a new plateau. It dawned on him that, if he didn't get out of the cage soon, he'd either die within it or be so physically fucked when he got free, he'd die within moments.

The School Girl shambled into the room, no doubt three to investigate the god-awful noise Tracy made. On closer inspection, Brendan estimated him to be in his sixties, the heavily wrinkled face framed by a Britney Spears pigtail wig. A hole gaped where most of his neck had been ripped out and the blood and gore soaked the white shirt and uniform tie beneath. The School Girl's mouth made snarling, snapping motions, but there was no sound. Brendan supposed that was from not having a voice box anymore.

He remained still so as not to attract the attention of their guest, but Tracy bit at The School Girl when he got close.

With Tracy distracted, Brendan made his move. He reached his fingers through the cage with one hand and gripped the lock, then brought the other hand up with the key. The pain in his neck and shoulders was excruciating, and he shook as he twisted his head to see what he was doing. He brought his hands together on the lock, willing Tracy not to notice his exposed fingers. *Almost there*, he thought.

The School Girl turned away and Brendan froze.

Tracy circled back to face him and stood still for a moment. With a snarl, she grabbed at his fingers, but he pulled them back to safety.

He registered pain as he ripped a layer of skin from his middle finger. Reflex pulled his hand close, and he dropped the key. It skidded across the floor and disappeared from his view. "Nooooo!" Brendan lost it. "Bitch! Cunt! You fucking whore!" he raged as he thrashed against the cage. A red mist descended, and he lost it for a time. He almost didn't notice the clank of metal on one side, but Tracy had stopped and turned toward it.

He got himself under control and looked around. One side of the cage had swung down and lay on the ground. *Mother-fucking, role-playing motherfuckers*, he thought. Of course, there'd be a safety mechanism for these fucks. Brendan's thrashing had released the hidden catch. He should have realized none of these cunts would keep anyone confined against their will, but this was not a headspace Brendan was familiar with at all.

Brendan and Tracy moved in the same instant. Brendan rolled to his side to escape the cage as Tracy launched herself at him. Luckily, for Brendan, she'd been on the opposite side of the cage to the escape hatch and tripped over the large obstruction. She smacked her head hard on the floor, giving him some time.

Brendan got to his feet at the speed of a spry septuagenarian. He couldn't straighten because of his long confinement, but he hobbled off, hunched over, as fast as his temporarily crippled body could manage.

Tracy gained her feet and pursued him.

Out in the hallway, he moved faster, his body becoming his own again. The place was a carnal house, as though they called in the butchers instead of painters and decorators. The stench of death hit him like a bat in the face.

Brendan couldn't remember if the front entrance was to the left or right. He had a fifty-fifty chance of being correct, so he went left. He navigated around sprawled bodies too consumed to reanimate, or maybe they hadn't got around to it yet. Uncoiled intestines snaked across the floor, fat tripwires that threatened to send him sprawling.

He felt, and heard, Tracy behind him but didn't dare look around. Up ahead was The Dildo Avenger, her massive strap-on swaying back and forth. Upon seeing him, she turned his way.

Great, just great. He picked up speed but, at the last moment, dropped and slid across the gore slick floor. He hit The Dildo Avenger's legs and she sprawled across him. The massive dildo flopped about like it was sentient, impressive to behold.

The Dildo Avenger barreled into Tracy, who couldn't have been more than a few feet behind Brendan. They hit the ground in a tangle of limbs, tearing and biting, each thinking the other was Brendan.

Brendan didn't stick around for photographs. He pushed through the double doors at the end of the hallway and came face to face with Dickhead, who lurched and pushed him back into the hallway. His foot landed on part of a liver and he slipped and fell hard, knocking the wind out of him. He sucked down a ragged breath before Dickhead landed on him.

Dickhead's mouth opened wide as he inched closer to Brendan's face, but Brendan got his arm between them and kept him away. Brendan knew he wouldn't hold him off for long; Dickhead had the weight advantage.

Brendan looked around, desperate for a weapon, and his eyes fell on The Dildo Avenger's huge, beautiful, fake cock. It flopped about wildly in the tussle with Tracy. He reached for it, but it slipped out of his hand. He grabbed hold of it firmly on the second attempt, gripping the shaft, and pulling with all his strength.

For a moment, Brendan thought the dildo was too firmly

attached to The Avenger, but a strap gave, and he pulled it free. The force of its release sent him and Dickhead rolling, and he used the momentum to get to his feet. He stood there, naked other than the gore caked on him, with the monstrous rubber cock in hand, ready to do battle with the rising Dickhead.

"Fuck this!" He threw the dildo at Dickhead's face, turned, and ran through the double doors. Relief flooded him at the sight of the front door just ahead. Aware of his nakedness, he grabbed a coat from a selection on a portable coat stand to the left. He threw it on as he bolted through the front door and into the night.

CHAPTER 5
HOOFING IT

Brendan crouched beneath the trees, the overhanging branches offering cover as he observed the road ahead. It was another minor road, one that would have seen sparse traffic in the world before. It was empty, as far as he could see, and silent as a grave, but he gave it a few more minutes just in case. They'd made slower progress than expected because of his caution, but he figured they were better off slow than dead.

He hadn't been by this way in years, but there were signs of change. Somebody had moved long abandoned vehicles off the road, and the vegetation didn't encroach as much as elsewhere.

His caution was driven by his need to know what and who lay ahead. The sort of people who survived the end of the world were mostly the wrong type; he should know.

Satisfied no immediate threat waited ahead of them, he waved Eoin and Lillian forward.

They crept to his position, unspoken questions in their eyes.

He didn't answer them. "Come on. Keep to the trees and off the road," he said.

"Seriously, Brendan? This is taking too long. We haven't seen a soul all day," said Eoin, a little too loudly for Brendan's liking.

"Doesn't mean they're not out there," said Brendan.

Lillian reached over and touched Eoin's arm. "Brendan is right, Eoin. We should be careful," she said.

Eoin nodded and followed Brendan.

Lillian fell in behind the two.

For fuck' sake, he thought. *Following her lead already?* Brendan was in a mood since the Jeep died; before that, really. He looked back at Lillian trailing behind Eoin. She was beautiful, the type of woman Brendan would have pursued before the world went to shit, but something about her didn't sit right with him. She was far too beautiful and together to have survived in what the world had become. And he didn't like the effect she was having on Eoin. *Hypnotized by pussy in a matter of hours*, he thought. *Fucking Eoin.*

———

Fucking Brendan, thought Eoin. He stared resentfully at the back of Brendan's head as it moved forward at a glacial pace. *It's too damned hot for this shit!*

They would have reached the town by now had they used the road instead of clomping through the bushes at its side. And for what? Nothing, that's what. They hadn't seen another living soul all day. Sometimes Brendan got right up Eoin's snot. He half suspected he was doing it to annoy him, or Lillian, or both. Eoin glanced around at Lillian.

She smiled when she noticed him looking at her, and he smiled back. He was certain Brendan envied the obvious rapport between them.

"Are you okay, Eoin?" said Lillian in a whisper close to his ear.

His heart skipped a beat, but he wasn't sure if it was from surprise or her proximity to him. He hadn't noticed that he'd stopped as he frowned at Brendan's still moving form. "I'm good," he said. "Just tired of this."

"I'm sure he has his reasons," she said.

Eoin grunted.

Up ahead, Brendan turned and motioned with his hand to move away from the road. Without waiting for a response, Brendan disappeared through the hedge.

"You'd think that cunt was in the army," said Eoin.

"He wasn't?" asked Lillian.

"The Scouts were as close as he got to active service," said Eoin. He thought for a moment. "Or *Call of Duty.*"

Eoin didn't know what Brendan did before the fucktard apocalypse. Brendan avoided the subject and ignored questions about his former life. Eoin got the picture and stopped asking.

They followed Brendan through the hedge and away from the road.

———

Lillian brushed past the last few branches of the hedge, careful that they didn't whip back at Eoin, and found herself in a field gone fallow that sloped gently downwards into a small valley. She could see similar fields adjoining this one and a patchwork of them in the distance, on the valley's opposite side.

Eoin stumbled out of the hedge, grumbling and cursing incoherently at the inconvenience, and ran into Lillian's back.

"Sorry," he said, stepping around her. He caught sight of Brendan who was further into the field, walking away from them. "Where's he off to now?" he grumbled, shaking his head as he followed.

Lillian stared after him for a moment before following. She welcomed the opportunity to study both men, but before she'd taken two paces Brendan stopped and raised his arm with fist clenched in what she assumed was a 'stop' gesture.

Ahead of her Eoin said, "What's he fuckin' at now?" but continued to where Brendan stood.

———

Brendan gritted his teeth at Eoin's comment but didn't rise to it. By some miracle, he remained calm as Eoin stomped up to his side after ignoring the obvious signal to halt.

"What's up?" asked Eoin in a bored voice.

One of these days, you little prick. One of these days… Brendan pointed to the far side of the valley.

A low, "Shit," from Eoin, but that was all.

Across the valley, an enormous dark cloud, impenetrable and swirling, traversed the patchwork fields. It wasn't on path to meet them, but it drew gradually closer. As it did so, they began to hear sounds from that direction. First, an otherworldly hunting horn, but beneath that there were faint screams as though a thousand souls were suffering through the most awful torture.

Brendan swore his heart stopped for an instant when Lillian began to speak.

"I saw it take a whole caravan of travellers once," she said. "The lead car had broken down and they were attempting a roadside repair."

Brendan sensed she hadn't finished. He didn't have anything to say anyway.

Lillian indicated the unsettling cloud with her chin before continuing. "It came out of nowhere, bearing directly down on them. It moves quicker than you'd think, up close. It bore down upon them and consumed everyone. The last thing I saw before it rolled over the last family was a mother putting a knife in her child's skull."

Silence from the three observers as the hunting horn continued to sound across the screams of the damned.

"A mercy," said Brendan after a while.

"That thing gets anywhere close to us and, I'm sorry, but I'm out of here. Every man for himself," said Eoin.

"You're a true hero," said Brendan.

"Look around. The time for heroes is long gone," said Eoin.

Brendan didn't reply. He didn't feel like he could argue.

———

Eoin relaxed as the unsettling cloud disappeared from view. Brendan shivered beside him, and Eoin was glad he wasn't the only one affected by the unnerving, unnatural phenomenon.

"Come on," Brendan said, and resumed leading them down the valley's slope.

Eoin didn't argue as he fell in step behind him. He attempted a reassuring smile at Lillian, but it felt strained. Lillian seemed lost in her own thoughts and didn't notice, which was okay with him.

Her story raised some questions for him, like how she managed to evade the cloud if she was close enough to witness the child's death. He'd ask her later if he got the chance.

Lillian followed a few paces behind him, and the subdued group continued down the sloping meadow.

———

Lillian followed Brendan and Eoin to a small stream at the bottom of the slope. The water babbled along, making sounds like they made her listen to during therapy sessions what felt like centuries ago. *For all the good that had done.*

She hadn't seen Brendan read a map all day, making her think he was familiar with the area. Finding the stream so far off the road backed up her theory.

"Ah, fresh water, that's lucky," she said, attempting to illicit a confirmation from the taciturn man. Brendan only grunted, not taking the bait.

"Best thing I've seen all day," said Eoin.

That wouldn't be hard, thought Lillian, still shaken by the eerie cloud they'd witnessed. She regretted not doing more to help the people in the caravan, despite being certain that any action on her part would have led to her demise. That hadn't been her most recent encounter with the cloud, but she'd kept that to herself.

She knelt by the stream and splashed cool water on her face. Surprisingly, its freshness managed to wash some of her memories away.

Eoin knelt next to her and mirrored her actions. He then cupped some water in his hands and drank deeply. "So sweet," he said.

Foolish, thought Lillian. She wasn't about to trust the water. Who knew what dying, mouldering thing lay upstream. She filled her canteen, then popped in a sterilization tablet. She shook it before clipping it to her belt again. She'd chance drinking it in thirty minutes.

Brendan didn't drink from the stream either. He filled a small pot and went about preparing a brew.

"Make us a cup, Brendan," said Eoin.

Lillian grimaced internally at Eoin's needy tone. *The lapdog is strong in this one when it wants something,* she thought. A mean-spirited laugh escaped her lips, quickly stifled.

"Something funny?" asked Brendan.

Shit! "Sorry. Just relieved to be in company after seeing that thing again," she said.

Brendan grunted.

What's with this guy? She wondered, not for the first time that day, if Brendan, and maybe Eoin too, were fucking with her. Was this grumpy arsehole and friendly lapdog thing a routine? If it was, they were pitch perfect at it.

Brendan finished the brew and shared it between three tin cups. He handed one to Lillian, and she took it.

"Thank you," she said, and sipped experimentally. The coffee was weaker than she liked, but she welcomed the sweetness. She held the cup close so she could savour the aroma.

Eoin grabbed his cup. "Thankee kindly." He produced a battered pack of smokes and took out the last cigarette. He crumpled the box and threw it over his shoulder. It landed in the stream and floated away.

"Really, Eoin?" asked Brendan.

Eoin lit his smoke and dragged deeply. Exhaled. "What? Not like anyone's around."

These two are geniuses or the two dumbest fucks I've ever met, she thought. Lillian was acutely aware of the watchers. Two of them. One behind and one keeping out of sight ahead, but not always the same two. They'd shadowed the three of them since morning, all through their distant encounter with the sinister cloud. In her opinion, the watchers were capable, professional, but not perfect, if you knew what to watch for.

Can't these two see them? Maybe the cloud had thrown her companions off. Or maybe they were a step ahead of her and watching for signs that she was aware of their shadows. Lillian eyed her compound bow and quiver beside her backpack. She'd be ready to move if their shadows did more than observe.

Brendan emptied the dregs of his coffee on the ground, signalling the end to their break. He accepted the empty cups from Eoin and Lillian and stowed them in his pack.

Lillian was ready to go immediately, but Eoin dragged his feet, muttering complaints under his breath.

Brendan was sick of Eoin's shit. "Eoin. You're up," he said.

"What?" asked Eoin, a deer caught in headlights.

"Lead the way," said Brendan. He turned to Lillian, "You in the middle and I'll take the rear." Something wasn't right. It had been niggling at him all day, and this change might give him the chance to work out what it was. It would also allow him to check out Lillian's ass without her noticing.

Eoin hesitated. He seemed uncertain.

Brendan looked at his watch. "Come on. We haven't got all day," he said, curious about what Eoin would do.

Eoin swallowed nervously and shouldered his backpack. "Fine," he said, and clomped back through the meadow towards the road.

Lillian trailed a few meters behind Eoin.

Brendan trailed the same distance behind her. He nodded appreciatively. She had a *really* great ass. *Like two puppies wrestling in a sack*, he thought. He wondered what it would look like stilled in death.

They reached the road, and Eoin stepped out of the tree cover without hesitation, stepping onto the road's surface.

"Are you sure about this?" asked Lillian from the trees.

Brendan thought she'd directed the question at him, but Eoin answered.

"Yeah, I'm sure. It's fucking dead around here," said Eoin. He readjusted his pack and started walking in the middle of the road.

Brendan thought he detected a soft sigh from Lillian before she stepped out after Eoin. Brendan gave it a few seconds before following them. He wasn't checking out Lillian's rear end anymore; he was frowning. Eoin had jogged something in his brain, and he realized what was bothering him.

They hadn't encountered even one undead all day.

———

Eoin led the way with a spring in his step. He didn't know exactly where they were going, but he'd get them there a lot faster than Brendan would have. He was sure Brendan would guide him if he strayed off the path, but for now, the road was straight, so it wasn't important.

They navigated a series of sharp bends that would have been dangerous if traveling by car. They still obscured the road ahead, for an uncomfortable few minutes, until the farmland to either side gave way to occasional bungalows and duplexes.

Eoin stopped before the first of them. It had smashed windows and the front door was off the hinges. Broken furniture, clothing, and other household items littered the front yard.

Lillian and Brendan joined him. "Should we check it out?" he asked.

Brendan shook his head. "Looks ransacked to me, but whatever you think."

"Let's keep going," said Eoin.

The group moved on, sticking close together rather than strung out in single file. All the residences they passed were in the same state of disarray.

Eoin wasn't worried; none of the damage looked recent. They passed a signpost that would have told him the name of the place they entered if it wasn't so faded. The clusters of former homes became more dense. It was deathly quiet as they passed the burned-out shell of a bar and restaurant on the right. A charred body lay half out of one window, crawling with flies. Eoin thought he could still smell the burnt meat in the air.

He was tense as they approached a Y-junction. He looked left and right, but one choice was as good as the other, so he turned left.

"Right," said Brendan.

Eoin didn't argue, just changed direction and walked on past looted shops on both sides. An old country church loomed on their left as they started up the small incline. Eoin was trying to think of something smart to say about God, or belief, or something, to lighten the mood, but he froze.

A man stepped onto the road thirty meters in front of them and levelled the double barrels of a shotgun at them.

"That's far enough, friends," he said. His voice was pleasant; his eyes were cold.

Eoin raised his hands slowly. A glance over his shoulder showed Brendan doing the same. *Where the fuck is Lillian?*

———

As soon as Eoin and Brendan took the right turn at the Y-junction, Lillian made her move. She stayed behind both men and kept close to the buildings on the right. It was a relief to shake the crawling sensation of Brendan's hungry eyes, never mind the Watchers.

When Eoin went left at the junction and Brendan had corrected him, Lillian slipped silently into a doorway. Inside, she stowed her backpack, taking only the compound bow and arrows. She crept through the abandoned building and exited into an overgrown backyard.

As soon as she stepped outside, a sharp coldness, enough to take her breath away, assailed her. It crept across her skin making it crawl and causing her to shiver. She recognized the Shadow's touch immediately and scanned the yard. *Where are you?*

She almost missed the undead child, overgrown with vegetation as it was, but spotted the swirling black pits it had for eyes. The child must have died on its tricycle and been unable to dismount when it turned, then nature gradually solidified its position. A stray Shadow must have claimed the body and become trapped within.

Interesting, thought Lillian. She'd been under the impression the Shadows had some foresight into the hosts they chose before entering.

Now, it looked like a garden sculpture with unnerving spirit eyes which followed her as she skirted the backyard. She kept as much distance between them as possible, unsure of the extent of the entity's power. As far as she was concerned, it could stay as it was forever.

Lillian climbed the five-foot wall at the rear of the yard and dropped into a back lane, little more than a footpath. She stalked back in the direction she'd come.

She saw the first watcher making his way along the wall towards her. He made so much noise, she had ample time to step behind a tree and draw her knife. She held her breath as he passed before snaking the knife around and stabbing him in the eye. His eyeball made a satisfying popping sound a split second before the blade scrambled his brain. She pulled the knife free as he crumpled to the ground.

She flicked the gore off the blade and continued.

The next one almost surprised her. He clambered onto the wall above her after coming from one of the other abandoned houses.

She reached up and pulled his legs from beneath him. His cry of surprise was cut short when his face connected with the wall. She saw cracked teeth and a shattered nose before he fell back into the garden. She followed him over and slit his throat open wide before he could regain consciousness.

"Night, night," she said, patting him on the cheek.

She retraced her steps and overshot the building where she'd stowed her backpack, swapping knife for bow as she went. The wall ended in a corner. She poked her head around it and saw the man still had the shotgun trained on Brendan and Eoin. He was talking to them.

"Where are ya comin' from?" he asked.

"South-east," said Brendan.

"Tara?"

"Nah. Bit further north."

"Stay clear of Tara. Fuckin' Shadows are bringin' their herds there from all over."

"We'll keep that in mind, friend," said Brendan.

The shotgun remained trained on Brendan and Eoin as the man nodded. "Ya don't know how lucky ya are," he said.

"Is that so?" asked Brendan.

No, you don't, Lillian thought, taking aim.

"Yeah, that bitch—" he began, but an arrow sprouted in his skull.

"What the fuck?" Eoin looked at the arrow all wide-eyed as Lillian stepped out of cover and walked over to the man's crumpled body. She picked up the shotgun and checked the chamber. Empty. She put it to one side and patted the man down but there was nothing of interest except a half pack of smokes. She tossed them to Eoin.

"Th-thanks," he said, with an awed expression.

Brendan stared at her hard. "Where the fuck did you go?" he asked.

She stared back at him. *You're fucking welcome*, she thought, but said, "Come on. There might be others." She jogged back to the building and retrieved her backpack before coming back and passing them without a word.

The two men were still looking at her as she walked past the church.

"I think I'm in love," said Eoin, poorly attempting a whisper.

"Shut the fuck up, Eoin," said Brendan, as he set out after Lillian.

Eoin shut up and trailed after them.

CHAPTER 6
DAY ZERO EOIN

BEEP! BEEP! BEEP!

Eoin rolled over and cancelled the alarm. The twenty-four-hour clock dial read 12:00 in a hellish red. Snoozing the alarm every ten minutes for the past hour had wiped him out.

He groaned as he sat up and swung his legs off the bed. He groaned again as he stood and looked around the bedroom for his clothes. They weren't in their usual spot, but he'd been drunk last night, and a little stoned, so who knew where he'd undressed?

He recalled Deirdre trying to get him up before she left for work in the morning, but she didn't succeed. That would have been at 7A.M. *What the fuck was that about? Did she say there was an emergency?*

As a policewoman, Deirdre worked long shifts of twelve hours, and often more, so he didn't expect her home for another eight. If there was an emergency, she could be away even longer.

Thinking of all that time to himself made Eoin smile. He checked his closet for a t-shirt and sweatpants, but he was out of clean clothes. He looked at his overflowing laundry basket and remembered arguing with Deirdre about chores. *What am I? Fucking twelve?*

It wasn't his fault he'd been out of work for six months. It was a misunderstanding that had gotten him laid off —he hated the word fired; it sounded like an execution. Anyway, just because Deirdre owned the apartment didn't mean she could dictate what he did with his time.

"Fuck you, Deirdre," he said, but looked around the empty room guiltily.

He picked a t-shirt out of his laundry basket and gave it the smell test. He winced; there was no fucking way he could wear that again. He tried a few more, and they were no better. His eyes strayed to Deirdre's empty laundry basket on her side of the room and then to her closet. A slight shrug and he was in there, raiding like a fucking Viking. He chose her favourite *Sex Pistols* t-shirt, along with a pair of pressed black leggings, and slipped them on. They were a snug fit and the fresh feel against his skin was wonderful. He'd put them back once he'd done his own laundry and Deirdre would be none the wiser.

In the kitchen, he went straight to the fridge to retrieve the pizza box from last night. He ignored the note Deirdre stuck to the fridge door at eye level containing a list of work items as long as his arm. He selected the two largest pizza slices and put them on a plate. After a sixty-second nuking in the microwave, he munched into them. *Breakfast pizza's the fucking best,* he thought.

He returned the remaining pizza to the fridge. He'd eat it for dinner if Deirdre wasn't back. When he closed the fridge door, he reviewed Deirdre's list of commandments. Unusually, it started with a note:

———

Hey Baby,

This is important, so pay attention. There's a national emergency and everyone has been called in. I don't know when I'll be back, but I have stocked the apartment so you should be good for a while. In the meantime, I need you to do some things:

1. Do your laundry - you have no clean clothing and the water supply might be interrupted.

 2. Make an inventory of supplies - food, water, medicine, and potential weapons.

 3. Keep the TV on a respectable news channel to keep abreast of developments.

 4. Stay inside, keep away from the windows, and don't let anyone in.

 5. Don't get stoned.

Love,

Dee

Eoin read it again. What the fuck? He wondered if Deirdre had finally lost it; maybe caused by the pressure of a high-stress job. Then, he suspected it was an elaborate ruse to make him do his laundry, but he was sure she'd have made something up to get him to clean the toilets, too. And the part about staying inside didn't sound like Deirdre at all; she constantly nagged him about not going outside enough.

Sitting down on the couch, he read the note a third time. He turned on the TV and chose a national news channel. It looked like all hell was breaking loose: people rioting and looting, police and army on the streets of Dublin, gunshots, burnt-out cars, buildings on fire.

"Fucking hell," he said. He switched around and channel after channel it was the same. Utter chaos outside and the repeated message to stay in your home.

He flicked back to the national news channel where a camera crew was transmitting live from the streets. The camera work was shaky as hell as they got into position at the edge of a building somewhere on the outskirts of Dublin. The camera leaned around the wall and took in the adjoining street.

"What the actual fuck!" said Eoin.

In the far distance, a building in ruins was surrounded by a cloud of dust and smoke. Within the cloud, something monstrous moved, indistinct but massive. The audio equipment captured the deep, otherworldly sound of a hunting horn.

"What the fuck is that?" asked a female voice off screen.

"No idea," said a male voice, closer, probably the cameraman.

"Move closer," said the woman.

"I don't kn—"

"Just do your fucking job," she said and moved into the shot. "Follow me."

Before she'd move more than a couple of paces, a shape made up of concentrated darkness shot from a side alley and knocked her off her feet.

The cameraman kept the woman and her assailant in shot as the darkness pushed into her.

She shuddered, slowly at first, but then more violently until it looked like she was having a fit.

The cameraman muttered, "Fuck this," and dropped the camera to the ground. The feed turned to static.

Eoin watched the static for a moment before turning off the TV. *What in the name of sweet Jesus was that?* He went to the book-case, retrieving his stashbox from behind his prized collection of graphic novels.

On the couch, he rolled a fat joint. "Don't get stoned?" he asked the empty room as he lit the joint. He inhaled and held it, then exhaled the thick smoke. "Fuck you, Deirdre."

———

Eoin peered from the edge of the curtains at the street below. He'd turned the apartment lights off so he wouldn't be thrown into silhouette. With eyes like dark pools, he searched for the source of the sounds he heard moments before.

He couldn't get what he saw on the news out of his head. Every shadow took on a menace of its own. He was sure the Shadow stalked him. Part of him, deep inside, knew he'd smoked too much and was stoned as fuck. This part knew the paranoia he felt was a result of his own over-indulgence, but what he'd seen on the television overrode that sensible part. So, there he stood, obsessively watching the street for signs of the Shadow coming for him.

Movement across the street.

A dark figure emerged from a doorway. His heart leaped until the shape solidified into a shambling drunk.

"Fuck!" He dropped down and sat with his back to the wall beneath the window. "What am I doing?"

His voice sounded like it wasn't his own. He needed to get out of the headspace he was in.

His eyes fell upon his stashbox, still open on the coffee table between the couch and TV. He stumbled upright and lurched towards it. Plucking out a baggie of coke, he went to work preparing a few lines with a store card he reserved for this purpose. He cut the larger lumps down as well as he could before rolling tight a twenty euro note.

Two long inhales saw the coke into his lungs. The fog lifted from his head.

"Fuck yeah!" he said, feeling one thousand percent better, all thoughts of Shadows left behind.

———

Eoin held the controller and stared at the TV screen as hordes of zombies rushed his character. He bashed the buttons frantically to fend them off with his improvised club.

"Take that, motherfuckers!" he shouted at the screen.

The volume was high, which almost drowned out the noise from the street outside. It got more chaotic out there as the day went by. He glanced at the clock over the TV. It read five o'clock. It would be dark in a few hours.

He looked in his stashbox, open on the coffee table before him; it was diminished since earlier. He swapped the controller for a rolled up twenty euro note and twisted it tight. A deep sniff and the cocaine entered his lungs. The numbness spread from the back of his nasal passage down the back of his throat. *That's it for the coke*, he thought.

He opened a small bag of pills next and swallowed down two with a swig of beer. The ecstasy would take effect in twenty to thirty minutes. He already felt the flutter of anticipation in his stomach.

Back in the video game, he killed more zombie hordes until he lost focus and zoned out. When the rush hit, it came with a world of possibilities. Restless, he turned off the game and switched on some music.

The noise of slaughter was replaced by summer dance tunes, and Eoin moved about the lounge with abandon. He sang along when he knew the words, transported back to parties and clubs where he'd first heard the music. He was buzzing. Remembering the beautiful ladies in the music videos prompted him to switch from Spotify to YouTube.

He stopped singing and dancing to focus on the stunner on his laptop screen. Suddenly, he was horny as hell. *Yeah, baby,* he thought as he felt another rush.

He had his dick in one hand as he navigated to a porn site with the other. Thinking of Deirdre, he searched for *'cop uniforms'*. He clicked on the first video in the results and as the scene unfolded, he dropped Deirdre's leggings and masturbated.

———

The clock over the TV read 7:30 and Eoin still masturbated. The dance music has stopped playing long ago and The only sound in the room was of the sex act playing out on his laptop screen. Outside was quiet, apart from the occasional explosion, gunshot, or scream in the distance.

Eoin's hair was damp with sweat, as was Deirdre's *Sex Pistols* t-shirt. His dick ached, but he kept wanking—he was close to cumming.

On screen, a sexy Catholic nun was being fucked hard by a psychotic clown. A pretty girl-clown, sporting a deranged look, fucked herself with a crucifix dildo. She reached orgasm and squirted a deluge over the nun's face as the psychotic clown withdrew his dick and anointed the sister with semen.

Eoin blew his load all over the laptop screen.

"What the actual fuck!?" asked Deirdre from the lounge door.

Eoin jumped up in shock and knocked the laptop over, mercifully closing the lid and silencing the ecstatic nun. He tried to move towards her as he pulled the leggings up but tripped and fell hard on the floor. "Deirdre," he said, looking up at her.

"Shut the fuck—" she paused. "Are you wearing my clothes?"

"Sorry, babes."

"Don't sorry babes me, you fucking waster." Deirdre looked around the room for the first time. She took in the empty beer bottles, the overflowing ashtray, the depleted drug stash and associated paraphernalia. "Are you high again?"

Eoin shrugged. "Seemed like a good idea."

Deirdre sat down on the couch and placed her head in her hands. She breathed in and out slowly for the count of ten before looking up.

Eoin felt self-conscious under her penetrating gaze, aware of his bare ass and cum covered hand.

"Did you do anything on the list?"

He grimaced and looked away.

"For fuck's sake," she whispered it this time.

"Sorry," he said.

"Save it." She stood. "I'll gather some things. You get dressed and clean yourself up. You look a fucking state."

Deirdre left him alone in the lounge and he breathed a sigh of relief. *That could have been worse,* he thought. He was still under the effects of the ecstasy he'd taken hours ago, but he was coming down. Glancing at the drug stash, he counted five pills in the little plastic bag. He shook one pill out and pocketed the bag. He drank a swig of beer and swallowed the pill before he had time to question himself.

———

Eoin felt amazing once the pill kicked in. He'd put a wash on, mostly his clothes, but what he'd worn of Deirdre's too. He changed into the least soiled jeans and t-shirt from his remaining clothes.

As he waited for the wash to finish, he followed Deirdre around the apartment as she inventoried their supplies. A pang of guilt struck him at not completing the task during the day, but it disappeared when he remembered how sound Deirdre was.

"I love you, Deirdre," he said.

She paused in counting the tinned goods and looked at him suspiciously.

"What did you take now!?" she asked.

"Nothing! You're just the love of my life, that's all," he said. He willed his mouth to look normal, but his jaw had a mind of its own and moved from side to side.

I'd murder someone for some chewing gum, he thought as he lit up another cigarette; he'd been chain-smoking in between gulping down hot, sweet tea. The tea was fucking lovely.

"Are you sure you don't want a cup of tea?" he asked, for the tenth time.

"No. I don't want a cup of tea, Eoin." She sighed. "Do you understand what's going on outside in the world?"

"Yeah, of course," he said. He hadn't a clue, having turned off the news early in the day and not gone back to it.

Deirdre's expression called him out as a liar.

"Fucking terrorists, or a revolution, or World War three?" *Maybe all three*, he thought, remembering some scenes.

"People are going crazy and killing and eating other people. Those murdered people are getting up and doing the same. Dead people are getting up again and going crazy too. There are even rumours of… a creature… in Dublin. It's a communication dead-zone in the city now. This could be the end of civilization as we know it, babe. Or it might be the end of days."

Eoin took a long drag on his smoke as Deirdre's words sunk in. He chose to ignore the religious connotations in her end of days comment. He was sure it was caused by the stress of a tough day. "The end of civilization?" he asked.

"The end of civilization," she confirmed, "or worse."

A broad smile spread across Eoin's face. "Guess I won't have to look for that job then."

Deirdre met the statement with stunned silence. Then she burst out, "Are you for real? This could throw humanity back centuries, or be the end of us entirely, and the first thing you think of is not having to work?"

He shrugged and took another gulp of tea.

"We might have to fight for food and water. We might have to kill other human beings, and that's being optimistic. This is no joke," said Deirdre. She was close to tears.

He went to her and enclosed her in his arms. "I'm sorry. It was a poor joke," he said, trying to calm her.

Her warmth felt good against his body. He felt his dick stiffening and hoped she didn't notice. As she cried into his t-shirt—he was grateful it wasn't clean—he sensed her relax as the tension melted away.

He hadn't been joking about the job situation, though; he'd trade fighting randos for resources and killing them if necessary for working in some dead-end job any day of the week. *Bring it on!*

No matter what Deirdre said of the dangers, Eoin wasn't worried. He knew he was safe with her. She was strong and resourceful and wouldn't let anything happen to him. She'd protect him.

"I fucking love you," he said.

A distant explosion shook the apartment. A moment later, the lights went out and they were plunged into darkness.

CHAPTER 7
PSYCHO BITCH COUNTRY

The sign read, '*BEWARE! PSYCHO BITCH COUNTRY!*' It was painted in a garish red on the side of a once-white Transit van on the outskirts of town.

"What the hell does that mean?" asked Eoin.

Brendan didn't know what the sign meant. It hadn't been there the last time he'd been through. "Just someone trying to fuck with us," said Brendan. By the look on Eoin's face, Brendan thought the tactic was working.

Lillian didn't look phased. "We should keep going," she said.

"Agreed," said Brendan. "This doesn't change anything. We still need to secure two rides and go our separate ways." He made sure he got that in as a reminder to Romeo Eoin.

"But what if it's something to do with the shotgun guy?" asked Eoin.

Brendan side-eyed Lillian as he answered, "Not like we can go back and ask him."

No reaction. Lillian ignored him. She started forward again, leading them on.

Brendan shrugged and gave an after-you gesture to Eoin.

Eoin set off too.

Brendan studied Lillian, as he'd been doing since she took out the shotgun dude. Whereas up to that, he had focused on her beauty and thoughts of what he would do to her. From then on, he noticed how she moved. She was lithe and efficient and took notice of everything in her environment. He wondered how good she was with the knife at her belt. Although he had the advantage of size, he thought he might still be outmatched if she was as fast and accurate as he perceived her to be. *An old-fashioned spiking for this one*, he thought.

He squinted at her and estimated her weight, then calculated how much Special K it would take to knock her out. Way less than they used to subdue the undead sluts.

Ahead, Eoin stopped to light a cigarette, drawing deep. He exhaled a cloud of smoke as Brendan passed.

"Watch it!" said Brendan.

"She's pretty amazing, right?" said Eoin, oblivious to Brendan's irritation.

"Yeah. Great," said Brendan, flatly.

"We should ask her to join us."

Brendan was stunned. Eoin often came out with stupid shit, but that was part of his charm. Brendan was finding out that puppy love, dumb-fuck Eoin, wasn't charming at all. "Are you out of you fucking mind?" he asked.

"What do you mean?"

Brendan fought to control himself. *Keep calm. Deal with this later.* He moved closer to Eoin and kept his voice low. "What do you think she'll make of what we do? You think she'll want to join in?"

Eoin hung his head. "No. But…"

"But what?"

"I've told you, man—" said Eoin, all serious.

"Oh, here we go."

"I don't want to do that shit anymore."

"The first bit of live snatch comes along and—" started Brendan, but Lillian noticed their heated discussion.

"Everything okay, boys?" she asked.

"Yeah, everything's fine," said Brendan.

"Lover's tiff?" she asked.

Eoin turned beetroot.

Brendan ignored her. "This isn't finished," he said to Eoin. "Now come on."

They continued towards town, but now Brendan watched Eoin and Lillian, thinking it might be time to put the cunt out of her misery.

———

Eoin saw them as they approached the old stone railway bridge that crossed the road ahead. They were about halfway down the gentle slope when he noticed movement in the shadows beneath the bridge. "What the fuck is that?" he asked.

Brendan took out the binoculars and focused on where Eoin pointed.

A low whistle. "Fuck me," said Brendan.

"Let me see," said Eoin.

Brendan handed over the binoculars.

"Jesus…"

Suspended beneath the bridge was a dense cluster of undead. Each one had their limbs and heads pierced with meat hooks attached to chains which suspended them off the ground. All were children, from toddlers to teenagers, and each was arranged in a unique, grotesque pose.

It's like a sick puppet show, he thought.

"What is it?" asked Lillian.

"Fucked up, that's what it is," said Eoin. He gave the glasses to her. Eoin watched as Lillian took in the fucktard puppet-show, waiting for her look of disgust. It didn't come.

"I think we can go under them," she said and handed back the binoculars.

"The fuck we can," he said, but Lillian was already moving towards the bridge.

The undead children became agitated as they approached. Their moaning was higher pitched than the adult undead, and it set Eoin's nerves on edge. *Creepy as fuck,* he thought and shivered.

Lillian got down in a push-up position to look under the undead children's feet. "We can make it." She stood and took off her backpack, got down again and, pushing the pack before her, crawled under the mass of emaciated, rotting legs.

Eoin looked at Brendan for confirmation that this was a terrible idea, but he already had his backpack off.

Brendan dropped to the ground and followed Lillian. "Come on. Don't want the missus thinking you're a pussy, do you?" Brendan called back as he crawled after Lillian, copying her technique.

"For fuck's sake," Eoin said under his breath, and took off his pack. There wasn't a chance in hell he was staying on that side on his own. He pushed and crawled, pushed and crawled, as he looked straight ahead at the others' feet. *Don't look up,* he thought. *Only a little more to go.*

A weight fell on his lower back from above. He froze but when whatever it was moved towards his head, adrenaline shot through him, and he crawled like a motherfucker. He ripped the skin from his hands as he pulled himself forward, but he didn't care. On the other side, he jumped up and shook himself spasmodically. "Get it off! Get it off!"

Lillian ran in and pulled something from his back.

He turned to see her holding a fucktard infant at arm's length as it strained to bite her. He doubted the few teeth the thing had would even penetrate her skin. Before he could rush in and help, Lillian took the thing by the legs and swung it to the ground. The force smashed its skull open on the tarmac, plastering the road with blood, brains, and little baby teeth. "Thanks," he said.

Lillian shrugged. "I put it out of its misery."

"Poor thing must have thought you were its mother," said Brendan.

"Fuck you," Eoin said, but his heart wasn't in it. *Baby fucktards are the absolute fucking worst,* he thought.

He looked at the road ahead of them and his mouth dropped open. "What the fuck is this?"

———

Brendan didn't know what the fuck this was, but he had a crawling feeling inside. *This isn't good,* he thought.

The road sloped upward from the bridge and along each side was a proper freak show. For as far as he could see, the undead stood at intervals on each side of the road. The ones closest to him were bound to lampposts and telegraph poles. They were stripped of all clothing and had something written on their chests. He moved closer for a better look.

"Be careful, Brendan," said Eoin.

He sounded nervous, and Brendan noted he had stayed close to Lillian. *The saviour,* he thought.

The one on the left lurched at Brendan when he got near, but the chain attached to a collar at its neck pulled it up short.

As Brendan edged closer, he noticed someone had removed its genitals. The wound showed no signs of healing, suggesting the removal was done after death. A wide slash-cut to its throat probably ended it. The writing on its chest read *FALLEN*. Someone had carved the word deep into the flesh. *That's fucking weird*, he thought. Brendan mused at the meaning of the word.

"You think he tripped over his dick?" asked Eoin, a light-hearted attempt betrayed by the quaver in his voice.

Brendan approached the one on the right and found the same restraints and the same castration, but with *PEDOPHILE* on its chest, again carved deep. The scarring to the wounds indicated they had been inflicted before death.

Looking further up the road, he could see similar placings until the road turned. *Who takes the time to do this shit?* He felt a thrill in his stomach at meeting them. Turning to the others, he said, "What do you make of this?"

Lillian shrugged.

"Between those kiddy puppets and this shit, I think we should turn the fuck around," said Eoin. "We're not dealing with normal crazy here."

"I've come too far to turn back," said Lillian. She shouldered her pack and set off along the middle of the road. Brendan stayed on the right, out of arm's reach of the rogue gallery.

A few moments later, Eoin moved out. "Fucked if I'm staying here on my own," he grumbled.

They rounded the curve in the road. Brendan had a clear view up to the town centre. The undead gallery of rogues continued, unbroken, on either side. As they moved closer to town, he could tell by the difference in their state of decay that the undead were more recently turned. The carved monikers varied, from vague to very specific. On his side alone, Brendan encountered a *SINNER*, a *GLUTTON*, a *DEFILER*, and a *MOTHER-FUCKER* along with a smattering of *CUNTs* and at least two *ASSHOLEs*.

Eoin let out a guffaw. "This one says '*RUDE*'. Like, what the fuck?"

"I saw one a minute ago with '*NOT A GOOD PERSON*'," said Brendan.

"Really? That's grasping at fucking straws, man," said Eoin.

Lillian stuck to the centre of the road and remained silent. She looked straight ahead, not glancing at what he and Eoin found so fascinating.

Brendan smirked at the woman's obvious discomfort. *Not as tough as you think, pretty lady?*

———

Lillian hid her irritation at Brendan and Eoin's juvenile comments. She kept her eyes on the tarmac ahead and continued walking. There was no need for her to look to either side. She remembered what each of them had done, as well as their names. Brian had been miles away from the good person he pretended to be so '*NOT A GOOD PERSON*' was a fitting label, and Michael had been exceptionally fucking '*RUDE*'. At the end, at least. Not as rude as you two, she thought. She had almost executed the two of them when they spoke about Gabriel, the '*FALLEN*' one. A smile twitched at the corner of her mouth, but she fought it down. There'd be plenty of time for smiling once she'd dealt with Eoin and Brendan.

Just like the rest of them.

———

A list was building in Eoin's mind as he walked the road into town. A list partially prompted by the names written in fucktard flesh he passed along the road. Eoin's list would contain all the snide remarks and insults Brendan sent his way over the time they'd been together. He was still puzzling out what Brendan meant about Eoin being the baby fucktard's mother, but he knew it wasn't complementary.

Eoin's skin crawled at the thought of it on his back. *Thank fuck for Lillian*, he thought, for the hundredth time. He could get used to her being around. He cast a sly glance her way, studying her from the corner of his eye: the sure movements and proud bearing. *Sexy as fuck*. She reminded him so much of Deirdre. A complex mix of nostalgia, remorse, and guilt washed over him. This prompted him to look at Brendan. *Smart-ass, pompous cunt*, he thought. There wasn't enough space on Brendan's chest to carve all those words. Eoin shied away from what words would be appropriate for his own chest. He told himself that most of the awful things he'd done were because of Brendan. Just like always, he almost believed it.

CHAPTER 8
DAY ZERO EOIN: DEIRDRE

Eoin and Deirdre embraced in the darkness for only a moment after the shaking caused by the explosion subsided.

Deirdre pushed away from him, drying her eyes on her sleeve. "That was the power station. Come on!" she said.

"Where are we going?" he asked. He was buzzing and just wanted to chill with her. Going anywhere wasn't part of his immediate future.

"It's not safe here." Deirdre left the lounge and came back moments later with two backpacks. She thrust one at Eoin. "Put this on," she said, putting on her own.

"But you only just got here, Dee," he said, and even to his own ears it sounded like a whine.

"Fine. Stay here," and she turned for the door.

"Wait!" he hurried after her, shouldering his backpack. He wasn't staying in the apartment on his own.

The landing was darker than the apartment. Eoin trotted to the elevator and pressed the call button.

Deirdre gave him a funny look and walked past him to the stairs.

"Fuck! Sorry!" he said, embarrassed he'd forgotten the power was out.

Deirdre only shook her head.

He promised himself he'd follow her lead from now on; at least until the ecstasy wore off.

The three-story descent was quiet, except for their feet and the muted street sounds. He never paid much heed to the hum of the florescent lights, but the absence of their noise grabbed his attention.

On the ground floor landing, he almost tripped over Deirdre, who squatted at a corner surveying the lobby ahead. "Sorry, Dee," he said.

"Quiet, for fuck's sake," she hissed.

Eoin crouched down behind her and tried to make himself sink into the ground. *Focus, focus,* he thought.

"It's clear. Come on," said Deirdre. She remained in a crouched position as she ran to the front door.

Eoin mimicked Deirdre's movements but felt like an eejit. He had no idea what he was doing. As he reached her, Deirdre opened the door and slipped out. Eoin followed.

"Where are we going?" Eoin asked in a whisper.

"The station," said Deirdre, as she scanned the street in both directions.

Eoin's eyes widened. *For the love of Christ,* he thought. The bag of pills in his pocket took on an extra weight and he was super aware that he was still pretty fucking out of it.

Deirdre saw his worried expression and matched it with a disgusted one of her own. "Nobody's going to give a fuck about how high you are, Eoin! Have you looked around recently?"

The venom in Deirdre's voice startled him and, for the first time, he looked around. The night was still, with groans and echoes interrupting a silence which spoke of the absence of human activity and the lurking presence of the undead.

The street displayed the chaos and devastation unleashed over the past twelve hours. Vehicles lay abandoned at odd angles. Some showed signs of recent use, doors left ajar and keys in the ignition, signs of frantic attempts to escape the encroaching terror, broken cars from which survivors escaped. Evidence of battles against the undead.

Fires fuelled by knocked-over bins and discarded debris punctuated the night with their glow. Flames danced with an eerie flicker, casting haunting shadows across the broken pavement. The acrid scent of smoke and burning materials permeated the air, mingling with the unmistakable stench of death.

To Eoin, the street was a chilling harbinger of the horrors yet to come. As the moon illuminated the devastation, he knew the world had changed. The true test of humanity's resilience had only just begun. "Fucking hell," he said. "What a downer."

He palmed another pill from the baggie in his pocket and slipped it into his mouth while Deirdre looked the other way. He used his spit to swallow it, almost puking at the harsh chemical taste. A better man might have felt guilty. *Fuck it*, he thought instead. *I can't be dealing with this shit.*

"Stay close to me. Don't fuck this up," said Deirdre.

That's a bit fucking cheeky, he thought, but he let it go. When Deirdre moved out, he followed close behind. "Would you look at these fucktards?" Eoin kept his voice low, as much to avoid another of Deirdre's dirty looks as fear of attracting unwanted attention.

They were half-way to the police station when they hit a snag: a group of twenty bloodied fucktards spread across the street, blocking their way. *Fucktards!* He was proud of coming up with the term all by himself, although he wasn't sure what he meant by it, only it suited the animated dead. He was fucked if he'd start calling them zombies. He didn't believe in zombies.

He was feeling pretty good again, his most recent ecstasy tablet taking effect.

To their right was a large supermarket; he had a brainwave. "We can go around them," he said, full of confidence as he fought the urge to chew his own jaw off. He pointed at the double-door supermarket entrance. *Finally! Chewing gum and a bottle of Coke!*

He could almost taste the spearmint and that sweet, sweet sugary beverage. He took the lead, hoping it would force Deirdre to follow him. It did; she fell in behind, albeit with a soured expression. He stayed close to cover, just as Deirdre had been doing, and made it to the doors without the fucktards seeing them.

———

The once bustling shelves stood depleted, stripped of dried and long-life goods. The air hung heavy with an unsettling stillness, broken only by the distant moans from the street and closer noises from the fucktards among the aisles.

Eoin steered Deirdre towards the candy aisle within the dimly lit confines of the supermarket. His heart pounded in his chest, a rhythmic symphony of fear and excitement as he scanned the desolate surroundings for packs of chewing gum, soft drinks, or other items. He'd scavenged a supermarket brand carrying bag when they entered, elated at not having to go with the cheap variety for a change.

Emergency lights flickered, casting eerie shadows which painted the scene in an otherworldly aura. As he crossed the main aisle from *Baked Goods* to *Snacks and Treats*, Eoin's gaze glimpsed movement.

Across the way, nestled in the shadows, a desperate family huddled in a corner, their eyes wide with dread. The mother, her face etched with anguish, raised a trembling finger to her lips, a silent plea. Then, she pointed to his right.

He peeked around the corner, and fear gripped him. Coming straight towards him were two child fucktards, one boy and one girl, both around twelve years old. At first, he thought they held hands, but on closer inspection saw cable-ties joined them at the wrists. He moved back before they spotted him. *Fuck! They're almost here!*

Deirdre was looking down the aisle in the opposite direction and hadn't seen the child fucktards, or the family, yet.

Eoin needed to act fast. Without taking his eyes from the cowering family, he reached out to the closest shelf. His hand sought blindly and grasped a lone jar. *This'll do.*

After a quick check that Deirdre still looked the other way, he launched the jar into the air with calculated precision. It exploded on the ground beside the cowering family. One child, a girl of around eight, let out a scream her mother tried to stifle.

Too late.

Time slowed as the child fucktards' vacant gazes snapped toward the tantalizing sounds. Their moans joined in a duet of bloodlust as they zeroed in on the promise of sustenance.

Eoin watched with a mixture of relief, horror, and disgust as the fucktards descended upon their prey. A multitude of emotions flooded him: relief that his ploy worked, horror at what was unfolding before him, and disgust at himself for instigating the slaughter.

"What's going on?" Deirdre whispered beside him.

He pointed at the family, frozen in terror as the child fuck-tards reached them, their hunger fuelling a dance of death and despair. Limbs flailed while screams of terror and anguish pierced the air, the symphony of life being torn asunder by the relentless jaws of the undead.

Deirdre moved towards them, but Eoin held her back.

"We can't help," he said. The last thing he needed was Deirdre rescuing them and hearing from them how he'd tried to save his own skin at their expense. They were beyond that now. Poor cunts.

Movement further down the aisle caught Deirdre's attention. More fucktards, drawn by the noise.

"This way," said Eoin, taking Deirdre's arm and guiding her away from the massacre. He was pretty sure he knew where the chewing gum was. And maybe, if he was lucky, he'd find a six-pack of cola. Something to wash another pill down with, he thought, as he tried to get rid of the sounds of the family being eaten. *That's a fucking downer…*

CHAPTER 9
DAY ZERO BRENDAN: SEX CLUB AFTERMATH

Where the hell am I? Brendan wondered. He crept through the front yard of the pop-up sex club house, holding his coat closed with one hand while he checked the doors of the cars he passed with the other.

He had agreed to wear a blindfold as Tracy drove them there that evening, a risk that thrilled him at the time. Consequently, all he knew of his current location was that it belonged to some rich pervert and was within a thirty-minute drive of his hometown. He could be anywhere.

The cars were all locked and he didn't dare break in to one for fear of what the noise would draw to him. The keys to Tracy's car were in her handbag back in the house and he had no intention of returning there.

He crouched behind the last car and tried to think. It was a frosty night, and the coat was his only protection against it. He needed to find something for his legs and feet, at the very least. A weapon would be good, too. *Anything but another giant dildo*, he prayed.

He crept to the front gate, an ornate, black-iron affair, and breathed a sigh of relief at finding it open enough for him to slide through. On the other side was a dark country road. He saw nothing that pushed him one direction over the other, so he took the left-hand path.

———

Brendan travelled the road for over a mile before he came to the next house, a two-room cottage which could have been lifted from the nineteen-fifties. The front was in darkness, so he hopped the low wooden fence separating it from the road and made his way to the back.

The back yard was in darkness too, but light came from a crack in the heavy curtain on one window. Brendan peered in and saw a quaint kitchen, lit only by a bright television screen. An old lady was seated on a comfy couch enthralled by one of those shaky-camera, found-footage, creature feature films. Something huge was laying waste to a city as people tried to flee. He didn't think he'd seen it before. *Weird taste, grandma,* he thought.

He turned back to the yard and saw a washing line. Closer inspection revealed a mix of old-fashioned men and women's clothing. He chose a pair of trousers and put them on; they were loose, but better than nothing. He took a pair of woollen socks and a light-coloured shirt and donned them too. Blood still covered his skin and marked his fresh shirt, but there was nowhere to wash that he could see.

"You look like you've been through the wars," said a voice behind him.

Brendan's heart almost stopped. He turned around and saw an old man sitting in the shadows. In his arms, he cradled an ancient shotgun. Brendan raised his hands. "Yeah, something like that," he said.

The old guy nodded towards where Brendan had come from. "Are you with them perverts?"

Conscious the man had seen Brendan steal what he assumed were his clothes, Brendan said, "I came from there. A bit too wild for me."

"Aye. A bit too wild everywhere tonight," said the man.

"What's been going on?"

The old man hawked and spat. "The dead walk and the Old Gods have returned to judge us," he said.

"Oh, yeah?" asked Brendan, thinking the old guy might be a touch senile. He shied away from the sex club massacre and the strange things he'd seen there.

The Old Gods? What the fuck? he thought.

"Don't suppose I could wash up inside?" he asked.

The man shook his head. "Nope." A pause. "But there's a tap

under the window that you're welcome to. You can keep the clothes."

Not that fucking senile. He went to the tap and turned it on.

"Is that you, Martin?" asked a wavering voice from inside.

"It is," replied the old man, Martin. "Stay inside."

"Okay."

Brendan went about washing himself. The water was freezing, but he scrubbed his hands, face, and hair as well as he could. The water turned dark as it flowed down the drain, taking pieces of offal and bone fragments with it. He was shivering when he finished.

Martin lifted an object from beside him on the bench. Brendan saw the glint of a hand axe. Martin placed it on the ground and slid it across to Brendan, who stopped it with his foot.

Brendan picked up the axe and tested its balance, a solid weapon. "Thanks," he said.

"Another mile and you'll reach the main road. Don't come back," said Martin.

Brendan nodded and left the old man to his watch.

———

The main road was just where Martin had said. A signpost at the junction pointed right for Brendan's hometown, but it was twenty-five kilometres away. He had no intention of walking all the way there, but started out anyway, despite the early niggle of blistered feet. *Got to keep warm.*

When a car neared, he raised his thumb, but it raced by. He couldn't say he blamed the driver under the circumstances. Four more cars did the same but, to his surprise, the next braked and pulled over. He walked the short distance to the passenger side before the good Samaritan reconsidered, affecting a disarming smile as he looked in the window. *Hello, pretty lady,* he thought.

"Picked a terrible night for hitchhiking," she said with a nervous, dimpled smile. She was mid-thirties, slim and pale complexioned with dark hair cut in a bob.

"Oh, I don't know. Weather's not bad," he said.

"Are you going far?"

"The next town. Twenty kilometres."

"Breakdown?"

"Yeah."

"I didn't see a car—"

"Turn left and drive for five minutes and you will," he said, a rueful smile this time.

She watched him for a moment, considering, then unlocked the door. "Get in," she said.

He opened the passenger door and hopped in, resting the hand axe on his lap.

"What's the hell!?" she asked in alarm.

"Oh, shit." He reached back and placed the weapon on the back seat, right next to a yoga mat. "Thought I might need it. The radio—"

She seemed to accept that and nodded. "It's like the end of days," she agreed. She drove back onto the road and the car settled into the quiet of random encounters.

Brendan wanted to know more about his new saviour. "I'm Brendan," he volunteered.

"Joan."

"Very pleased to meet you, Joan."

Another dimpled smile.

"Thanks for stopping," he continued.

"Don't make me regret it," she warned, half joking.

No comment, he thought. "What brought you out?" he asked, hoping he wasn't being too intrusive.

"I'm checking on my mum. I've been calling all night but she hasn't answered, so…" she gestured at the road ahead.

"Are you close?" he asked. A professional curiosity.

"Her house is a little way past your town. I've been driving for two hours," she said.

"Jaysus." *You'd drive to Galway in two hours!* "Do you need help?" he asked and nodded at the back seat. "I have an axe."

She laughed, "I might take you up on that."

CHAPTER 10
DAY ZERO EOIN: THE STATION

Deirdre took the lead after the supermarket. They left by a side door which allowed them to circumnavigate the group of fucktards in the street.

Eoin found a box of spearmint gum, a six-pack of wheat-beer, a bottle of coke, and some peanuts on the way out. As far as he was concerned, the detour had been a resounding success, but he didn't get the impression Deirdre felt the same way.

Eoin had already compartmentalized the slaughter of the family; filed under *necessary evil,* or *better them than us.* Deirdre focused on getting them to the police station, but Eoin was sure they'd talk more about the supermarket later.

They rounded the corner before the police station and noticed an immediate change. The street was empty of vehicles, and someone had erected makeshift barricades. Bodies lay away from the fortifications, dropped by some sort of ranged weapon.

Eoin couldn't see anything obvious that could have done it.

Deirdre raised her hands as they got close to the barricades, and Eoin followed her example.

"Slowly, and no sudden movements," she whispered to him, then raised her voice, "Deirdre Staunton. Garda Deirdre Staunton reporting for duty."

"Dee!" a bellow from above and a sporty-looking type wearing police issue riot gear stood up on a rampart. "Who's the damp squib?"

Eoin coloured at the insult.

"This is my boyfriend Eoin, Sergeant," she said.

"Ooooh! Boyfriend, is it? Well, let me know when you want a real man." He laughed at his joke like he invented humour, and Eoin heard a few laughs echo from within.

"Can we come in, Sarge?" she asked.

"Course you can, Dee. You can even bring the squib."

The heavy barrier moved out of the way, and Eoin and Deirdre walked through.

An older man with salt and pepper hair and a well-groomed moustache, aided by a young man who couldn't be long out of his teens, pushed the barrier closed behind them. Both men wore the same police issue riot gear as the sergeant on the rampart.

"Don't mind him," said the older guy with a grandfatherly smile that Eoin immediately warmed to.

"Yeah, he's been a prick all night," said the young guy, then added, "More than usual, like."

"Hey, Dan, hey Peter," said Deirdre. "This is Eoin."

They gave him a nod and a smile.

Eoin figured the old guy was Dan and Peter was the kid-cop. "Hey," he said, trying to be cool and not act like he was about to eat his own face from coming up on the ecstasy. He avoided eye contact with them. *My fucking eyes must be as big as saucers*, he thought, feeling a niggle of paranoia. "Where's the toilets?" he asked.

"Inside," said Dan. "Dee can show you."

Deirdre led the way around a makeshift barrier. "Are you alright?" she asked.

"Yeah. Yeah, I'm grand."

"Don't let Sargent Mooney bother you. He's a wind-up merchant."

"I won't." Eoin felt better, and a wave of appreciation washed over him. *I fucking love this girl; there's no-one in the world I'd rather be with tonight.*

Deirdre led the way through the front door of the police station.

———

Eoin washed his face in the sink in the police station restroom. The sensation of water on his face felt wonderful and, as a bonus, it took off the grime from the street. He dried himself with paper towels from a dispenser, then looked at himself in the mirror.

Fuck.

Even a half-wit would know he was on something, he'd never fool a bunch of rozzers. "Fuck it. What are they gonna do? Arrest me?"

He smiled back at the maniac in the mirror before popping a fresh stick of gum in his mouth. He considered the remaining pills in his pocket but decided against taking another one. Way too many police for that; he wouldn't enjoy himself.

He left the restroom and went back to the cells. That's where they were staying, the fucking cells. *At least we can leave the door open,* he thought.

As Eoin approached his and Deirdre's cell, he heard voices, so he stopped to listen. Deirdre and Mooney were talking about him.

"He has to pull his weight if you want him to stay, Dee," said Mooney, all reasonable.

"Yes, Sarge. But the evidence room?" she asked with a hint of incredulity.

"Somebody has to do it, and we're short on people," he said.

"Okay…"

"Is there any reason he can't go in there? Unduly squeamish, is he? Or something else?"

What's this cunt playing at? Eoin started moving and gave a cough before entering the cell.

"Ah, there he is," said Mooney. "I have a job for you."

"Oh, yeah?"

"Yeah. I need you to go through the evidence room and grab anything useful. Weapons, mainly, but anything else that might be of use."

He held out a set of keys to Eoin.

"Weapons?" asked Eoin. "Isn't there an armoury?"

"Ah, yeah. Long story. But the short of it is we can't get into it."

"You can't?" asked Deirdre.

"Yep. It's locked," said Mooney. The cunt didn't even have the grace to look embarrassed by the statement. "So, we need someone to go through the evidence room while the locked armoury problem is being worked on." He jangled the keys.

Eoin looked to Deirdre for advice, but she shrugged, so he took the keys.

"Evidence is in the basement. You can't miss it. It says 'EVI-DENCE' on the door."

Eoin turned and left, feeling relieved about spending the next couple of hours in his own company and not being watched by cunts like Mooney.

———

The evidence room was twenty meters square, with floor to ceiling shelves on three walls and a middle double shelf which created two aisles. A table and four fold-up chairs stood at the door end. Boxes, brown paper bags, and clear plastic bags filled the shelves, all numbered in a system that Eoin couldn't decipher.

The prospect of rummaging through the room's contents exhilarated him. He deduced that if the cops had grounds to seize something, it was likely something valuable. Eoin frowned. Why had that Mooney cunt given him the task and not a cop who knew the system? *Fuck it. Don't knock a gift horse, and all that.*

He lifted the first box from the top of the left-most row of shelves and brought it to the table. Inside were documents, arranged in folders, and three cassette tapes. *Fucking cassette tapes?* Had he tripped and fallen into the eighties? He returned the box and picked up the next. It contained more documents, along with biological samples. His heart lifted at the tightly wrapped bundles of cash in the third box, but then he remembered the shit show the world had become overnight. *Does it even burn?* He filed the thought away for future experimentation.

He discovered a small bit of marijuana in one bag along with personal effects, presumably confiscated during an arrest. That went in his pocket, of course, with his baggie of pills. More useless documents and assorted evidence, then a folding lock knife with a four-inch blade that looked serviceable. He put that in his back pocket.

Fifteen boxes in, he found a disassembled handgun in a clear plastic bag, but no accompanying ammunition. He turned the bag this way and that, undecided. *Is this useful?*

He returned the box to the shelf and picked up the gun part puzzle. Deirdre would know how to reassemble it, and maybe even know where to get ammo for it. He left the room, locking the door behind him.

Eoin was almost to their cell when he heard Mooney, "That's right, take that cock, you bitch," he said.

When Eoin got to the door, he froze. Mooney was between Deirdre's spread legs, his hairy ass pumping for all it was worth.

"What the fuck?" asked Eoin.

Mooney looked over his shoulder without stopping. "Back so soon, squib? Get lost for another five minutes. That's a good lad." Then, he turned back to what he was doing.

Eoin didn't know what to think. He couldn't believe Deirdre would do such a thing. She'd always told him Mooney was a creep who was constantly propositioning the female police officers. Had that been lies to cover up an affair? His stomach dropped as his world crumbled. He turned around and dropped the bag of gun parts on the floor before passing through the door.

"Close the door after you," said Mooney.

"Eoin—" said Deirdre, faintly before a slap cut her off.

"Shut the fuck up," said Mooney.

Eoin stopped with his hand midway to the door, "Deirdre?" She sounded groggy. He turned back and pulled the folding knife from his back pocket. The next moment, the knife was open and he stood behind Mooney. He registered a smear of blood on Deirdre's leg before he looked around the large police Sergeant's back to his girlfriend's face.

Mooney had clamped her mouth shut with a massive hand.

Deirdre's eyes were wide. They pleaded for help.

A red haze descended on Eoin. He stabbed Mooney in the neck, slicing into the artery. A fountain of blood spurted out and decorated the cell wall.

Mooney put his free hand to his neck to stem the flow. "What the hell?" he asked, looking surprised.

"Rapist cunt!" Eoin yelled before he slashed down, bringing the blade across Mooney's face.

The cut was deep, slicing into the man's right eye, bursting it, and opening a flap of skin on his cheek. The jelly from his eyeball flowed into the cut and mixed with blood as it entered his mouth through the flap.

Eoin next stabbed Mooney's gut, aiming at where he thought the kidneys were. Once, twice, his hands were drenched in blood.

Mooney floundered about and caught Eoin on the side, slamming him hard into the wall.

Eoin was stunned for a moment but came out of it in time to duck beneath the next blow. He came up next to Mooney's exposed penis, still half erect. Eoin grabbed it with his left hand and pulled it taut.

A look of terror flashed in Mooney's eyes as he mouthed a silent, "No."

Eoin sliced down with his blade, taking the head off. Mooney screamed as Eoin flung the severed piece to one side. He lifted the knife, prepared to end the man's miserable life, but a shaken Deirdre stood up behind Mooney.

She held out her hand and Eoin passed her the knife. She pulled Mooney's head back and drove the blade and half the handle deep into the remaining eye, burying it in Mooney's brain. The scream cut off and Mooney toppled to one side, landing hard on the cell floor.

Eoin stepped over him in time to catch Deirdre as she fainted. He lay her back on the bed, covering her as best he could. He heard a murmured, "Thank you," before she fell unconscious.

Eoin sat back on the bottom of the bed and caught his breath. He looked around at the bloody scene. "Fucking hell."

He looked from a sleeping Deirdre to the unmoving Mooney and back again. How was he going to explain this to the other police officers? *Maybe they're in on it.* The more Eoin thought about it, the more it made sense. Nobody came to investigate the noise from the cell; of course, they were in on it. *Fucking cops*, he thought. They stuck together no matter what.

He got up from the bed and went to Mooney's body. Stepping on his neck, he yanked the knife out of the cop's eye socket. He wiped the gore off on the already bloody uniform before leaving the cell.

Eoin made quick work of the rest of them. They didn't expect an attack from within.

He found Peter, the kid-cop, in the bathroom. He slashed his throat when he left the cubicle after taking a shit. At least he didn't soil himself.

Old-guy Dan was taking a nap; Eoin bludgeoned him to death with his own night-stick, finally satisfied he was dead when Dan's face was a concave mess.

Outside, a new guy watched the street from the rampart. Eoin didn't know his name but brought him a piping hot coffee and clambered up to give it to him. "Complements of Mooney," he said, as an explanation.

"Ta," said the cop. He sipped at the beverage, nodding appreciatively.

"Much about?" asked Eoin.

The man pointed at the shuffling forms of two fucktards beneath them.

"Aren't you worried?"

"Nah," said the man. "We're safe—" his words cut off when Eoin threw him off the rampart. The man landed awkwardly, and a crack of fractured bone sounded out, followed by the man's screams.

The fucktards moved in. One started on his fingers and another biting the flesh from his face.

Eoin turned and left the man to his screaming. Back inside, he dragged Dan's body to the evidence room. He returned to the bathroom to do the same with Peter's body, but it wasn't where he'd left it. He saw bloody footprints leading to the bathroom door, so he followed them out the door and down the corridor, his heart beating ever faster. *No, no, no.*

He followed the footprints into the cells and a sense of impending doom descended upon him when the prints led to the cell he shared with Deirdre. He wanted to run, but he couldn't make his body move fast enough. All he managed was a funereal pace.

In the cell, leaning over Deirdre, Peter the fucktard feasted. Sickening sounds of skin and meat being ripped from her body echoed in the confined space.

Eoin, oblivious to the danger, strode into the cell and yanked Peter's head back in imitation of what Deirdre did to Mooney only recently. He plunged the same knife into Peter's brain through his right eye.

Peter the fucktard dropped lifelessly over Deirdre's twice-ravaged corpse, but Eoin dragged him off her to lay him on the cell floor beside his Sergeant. He returned to Deirdre and knelt beside her, softly cradling her hand in his own. His voice cracked as he said, "I'm sorry, Dee." The apology broke something inside him, and he sobbed uncontrollably.

CHAPTER 11
DAY ZERO BRENDAN: JOAN

Joan took the ring road to bypass his hometown on the way to her mother's place. Brendan didn't mind. He was curious what had become of the old bird and how Joan would react if it wasn't good.

The house was a moderate two-story set in a well-maintained garden. Brendan could picture Joan growing up there, never wanting for anything, and he supposed that had paid off for mum as Joan was there now, checking up on things when all hell had broken loose.

"Something's not right," said Joan.

As they approached, they could see all the ground floor lights were on, and the curtains were open. There was no sign of life inside or out.

Joan parked close to the front door and they got out, Brendan remembering to take the hand-axe from the back seat. The gravel crunched underfoot as they walked to the door.

"Mum?" Joan called out as she unlocked the door and pushed it open.

Brendan stopped her with a touch to her arm. "Me first," he said.

Joan stepped aside and allowed him to enter before her.

He did so and quickly cleared the downstairs rooms while Joan followed. Back at the entrance, he looked up the wide stairs. "Which room is hers?" he asked.

"Second door on the left," she said.

Brendan nodded and led the way up the stairs and to the door. He brought his ear close to listen, but only silence greeted him from inside. With a firm grip, he lowered the handle and pushed the door open. A gasp came from behind him, and Joan rushed past.

She went to her mum, who lay on top of the bedclothes, facing the ceiling.

Brendan thought she was as dead as a doornail; you rarely see that pallor on the living. While Joan checked for vital signs, Brendan saw the empty bottle of pills and glass of water on the bedside cabinet. Both spoke volumes, but Joan wasn't listening to them yet.

"Mum? Mum? Wake up mum!"

Brendan heard the note of panic in Joan's voice, and this was before she figured out her dear old mum topped herself. He acted before that, thinking; *I don't need the drama.* Two quick steps brought him within arm's reach of Joan. Using the axe handle as a club, he pummelled her head.

She cried out and reached back in surprise. He struck her again, and she fell forward on top of her dead mum.

He found belts in the wardrobe and used them to tie up Joan. He left her on the bed with her mum while he went back down-stairs to see what there was to eat. It had been a long night, and he was fucking starving.

———

Brendan took another bite of his sandwich. It had ham, cheese, tomato, lettuce, and pickle on two thick slices of fancy wholemeal bread. *I'm having another one of these,* he thought.

He heard a thump from upstairs, like something falling off the bed. "Fuck," he whispered. *Awake already?* He was counting on Joan to be out for hours after the blow he'd administered.

Another noise. It sounded like someone dragging themselves across the floor. With genuine disappointment, he put down his half-eaten sandwich and picked up the hand-axe.

He dashed into the hallway and took the stairs two at a time, pausing at the bedroom door. Sounds of movement on the other side. He opened the door and rushed in.

Seated on the floor opposite, leaning back against the wall, Joan was attempting to stem the flow of blood from a gaping wound in her neck. Her eyes were wide with disbelief, her lips parted as though on the cusp of speaking.

"What the fuck!?" Brendan couldn't comprehend what was happening, but the penny dropped when he noticed the empty bed.

A second later, Joan's mum moaned and got up from the floor on the far side of the room.

Brendan sprang into action. He leaped onto the bed, then off it, barrelling into the old, dead woman with the momentum. This brought her back to the floor. There was a satisfying crunch when he landed on her chest. She clawed at his sides and arms, undeterred, so he hacked into her with the hand-axe. Each brutal strike cleaved off pieces of face and skull. Half a dozen blows later saw her head cracked open and her blood and brains spread across the carpet. *A bad day at the butchers*, he thought.

He looked around at Joan. Her breaths were shallow; she was fast fading. Brendan was disappointed he wouldn't get to play with her on his own terms, in his own time. *She's not dead yet*, he thought, feeling himself stir.

He dropped the axe and went to Joan. He dragged her back to her mother's deathbed, ripped off her jeans and panties, and positioned her belly-down on the edge so her ass was level with him. Her lifeblood continued to flow, soaking into the floral duvet. His breathing deepened as Joan's breaths became shallower. Dropping his trousers, he spat on his hard dick for lubrication, and entered her. She was tight around him; her dying body constricted. His grunting filled the room as he fucked her. He was so consumed with rutting like an animal, he didn't realize her breathing had stopped.

Brendan was close to orgasm when Joan moaned and moved again. It was subtle at first. He thought he'd imagined it, but she became increasingly agitated until she bucked at him, trying to get him out of her. He leaned into her and gripped her by the front of her shoulders from beneath her armpits. He pulled her to him as he exploded inside her. "Fuuuuuck!" he cried and collapsed onto the resurrected Joan. After his orgasm subsided, the reality of the situation hit him.

Joan continued to buck beneath him.

Brendan held on for dear life, his flaccid penis slipping out and flopping around wetly. She was strong. *Shit! What do I do?*

The hand-axe was on the floor beside the mother's corpse.

The door was closer, but on his other side. He chose the door. After a quick count to three, he pushed Joan onto the bed as he pushed himself off her. He reached down and pulled up his trousers, holding them tight at the waist as he dashed for the door. Once through, he pivoted and pulled it closed behind him before Joan regained her feet. A moment later, she slammed into the door. For one terrifying moment, he thought the door wouldn't hold, or she'd somehow turn the handle and step through, but the noise subsided. *Out of sight, out of mind?* Whatever the reason, he'd take it.

He dragged a dresser from what looked like a spare bedroom down the hall and positioned it in front of the door. The door opened inward, but he didn't think she could use the door handle or climb the dresser.

He leaned on the dresser gathering his thoughts. He needed a shower or a bath. The wash in the old man's yard had been cold and not very effective. He would look for some clean clothes to change into and a bathroom, in that order. *Please let there be hot water.*

———

An hour later, Brendan was back in the kitchen eating another sandwich. He was squeaky clean and wore a loose pair of sweatpants and a knit sweater scavenged from the hot-press upstairs, vast improvements over the old man's gear.

The occasional bang or shuffle came from above, but he was used to it, and it reassured him Joan was where he left her. He contemplated what he would do with her as he finished his food.

Exhaustion hit him as he went back upstairs to the spare room. He closed the door and locked it, then flopped onto the bed without undressing. The tension left his body as soon as his head hit the pillow.

He thought of work in a few days and his mood sank, but then it occurred to him that there would be no more work. A smile spread across his face.

I'm free!
No more office politics,
no more bullshit job,
no more inane conversations,
no more fucking meetings,

no more not giving a fuck about quarterly results,
no more performance reviews.
The world has died, and I've gone to heaven.
Brendan drifted into a deep sleep with the gentle thumping of Joan's resurrected body hitting the wall a few doors down.

———

The next morning, Brendan woke stiff-limbed but refreshed. Joan still rhythmically thumped on the bedroom wall, and Brendan briefly considered fucking her again. The risk versus reward was disproportionate, so he left her be.

He plundered Joan's mum's house for food, water, and a few other items. He left the house with two holdalls which he loaded into the boot of Joan's car. He had enough food and water for a week, but he needed footwear, more practical clothing, medical supplies, and a decent weapon. The best the house had to offer was a kitchen knife, a claw hammer, and an old hurley stick he found in the garage.

Getting into the car, he considered the day ahead. His next stop would be the town he'd bypassed the night before with Joan. It was moderately sized with two shopping centres, a hospital, a sport supply store, and a police station. He'd hit the police station first. *Bound to be weapons there.*

His eyes drifted to the meagre collection of weaponry on the passenger's seat as he pushed the key into the ignition. He hoped the police would part with some of theirs voluntarily. If not, he was confident he could persuade them.

He started the car and pointed it towards town.

CHAPTER 12
PSYCHO BITCH

Brendan stared at the chained undead from his position in the middle of the road. The final body before town stood out from the rest, but he couldn't put his finger on why. "Poor bastard," he said.

It kneeled with its lower legs beneath it and leaned against the railing it was chained to. It reminded him of an abused dog he knew when he was a kid, regularly starved by its owner and never seeing a day free of beatings. Brendan snuck into its yard one night to put it out of its misery. The dog didn't so much as whimper as he rained down blows with the crowbar.

The pathetic zombie in front of him had a different pallor to the others, a less green and more greyish tone. Even kneeling as it was, Brendan saw the healed scar where it had been castrated, but this one had a pinkish tone as though it were fresh. The way it was positioned obscured the words carved into its flesh.

"What the fuck is wrong with it?" asked Eoin, coming up behind him.

Brendan shrugged, "Don't know." He moved closer for a better look at the chest carving, but stopped out of arm's reach.

The words *'CHILD-KILLER'* were etched into its chest, looking healed but pinkish.

There was no response to Brendan's proximity, so he picked up a small stone from the ground and threw it at the creature.

When the stone hit its cheek, the head lifted and turned to Brendan as a drawn-out groan escaped its lips.

Brendan held fast, but when its eyes met his, he panicked and scrambled backward. "Fuck! He's still alive!"

The eyes were a clear blue, untouched by the usual undead milky film. A human intelligence burned there.

"The fuck it is," said Eoin.

"Look at his eyes."

The non-zombie raised an emaciated arm, finger pointing behind Brendan and Eoin, a look of recognition in his eyes.

"You—" the non-zombie started before an arrow flowered from his skull. He dropped back to his leaning position, fully dead.

Brendan spun to see Lillian lower her bow.

"Jesus, Lillian, like what the fuck?" said Eoin.

"He's better off dead," she said with a shrug.

"He knew you," Brendan said, certain of it as he spoke the words.

"I doubt it," she responded. She shouldered her bag and moved past the two of them.

"Why is that?" asked Brendan.

She paused and looked him in the eye. "Because I don't have time for child killers."

It took a moment, but when the penny dropped for Brendan, it dropped hard. *How did she know what was carved on his chest?*

Brendan watched Lillian walk away. Then he turned back the way they'd come and looked at the mile of bound, tortured men. *Did she do all this?*

Brendan's stomach dropped at the scale of it. This was his hometown and there was none of this the last time he was in the area. He was certain Lillian wasn't working alone. He cursed himself for letting his suspicion out. The last thing he needed was this psycho bitch being prepared when he made his move. He thought of the prepped ketamine dose in his backpack and figured he had half a plan.

Brendan turned to Eoin who still looked at the dead child killer with disgust and fear. *Can I trust you, Eoin?* Brendan moved to his long-time companion and put a hand on his arm to turn him away. "Come on, man," he said.

———

Eoin's mind still reeled at the shock of the fucktard not being a fucktard at all, but some poor, tortured cunt. "Who would do that, Brendan?" he asked as his friend led him away.

Brendan hesitated before whispering, "Maybe the same one who didn't want him talking."

Eoin stared back at Brendan. *What's he on about now?* he thought, then realization dawned. "No! Lillian?"

"Keep it down!" Brendan hissed at him.

Eoin watched Lillian as she walked ahead of them, out of earshot he hoped, so confident and sexy. "It couldn't be Lillian," he said.

"Why not? Because she has a nice ass?"

"Yeah. I mean, no." Eoin reined in his scattered thoughts. "Because there are hundreds of them and… she's a girl." When he heard himself vocalize it, he realized how lame it sounded. "What do we do?"

"Act normal," said Brendan. "Take her out first chance we get."

"Okay. Yeah."

As they continued, Eoin tried his damnedest not to look at Lillian's back as though he were watching a bag of snakes.

CHAPTER 13
FUCKING EOIN

Eoin lay beside Deirdre on the compact cell cot, just on the edge of wakefulness. She moved her ass against him in a way that drove him wild, and he felt himself stirring. The muted groan coming from her cloth-gagged mouth was strangely comforting. With his eyes closed, his drug addled brain believed nothing had changed between them. He felt himself get hard as she moved against his dick, faster and faster. "For old time's sake, eh, Dee?"

He gripped the top of her pants and pulled them down. Her body was a darker hue on the side closest to the floor where the blood gathered, but she was still sexy. He took his dick out and stroked it, then spat on it for lube. Angling himself for penetration, he had a couple of false starts without Deirdre's guidance, one of which he almost entered her ass.

He said, "Sorry," as if she would care.

He entered her cool, dank pussy on the next attempt and humped her for all he was worth. The sweat beaded on his forehead as she thrashed with renewed effort to reach him. "You know you want it, Dee," he said, but deep down he knew she was past wanting anything from him again.

———

Brendan crept toward the police station, hurley stick in hand. It was his second stop in town. After enduring the discomfort of driving barefoot, he made a detour to procure some necessary items. A shoe-shop provided a decent pair of hiking boots, while a clothing store gave him dark casual wear.

The undead dotted the street, but there were no large groupings. He used the improvised barricades as cover as he approached the police station's front doors. He stepped over the remains of a cop who lay before a large barrier. The cop moaned and reached for his leg, but Brendan crushed his head with a booted foot. Pieces of brain stuck to his shoe and the bottom of his jeans. He was glad he picked up a couple of spare pairs.

There was no way around the barrier, so he put his shoulder against it and gave it a shove. It shifted half a foot after some effort, so he put his back into it and created enough space to move through.

He paused on the other side to listen. All was silent, so he pushed the barrier back in place; he didn't want any surprises when he returned. Creeping forward, he noticed the front doors were open a crack. He entered and secured the door behind him.

Inside, he shouted, "Hello?" but not too loudly in case his voice carried. Eliciting no response, he crept from room to room on the lookout for lurking cops. He readied an excuse to explain his presence should he bump into anyone.

Brendan found a bloodied police baton next to a mess of dried blood mixed with pink pieces of brain and white bone shards. He followed a smeared blood trail through a door to a narrow corridor. The trail stopped at another door marked '*EVI-DENCE*'. He tried the handle, but it wouldn't open.

Retracing his steps to where he found the baton, he discovered bloody footprints leading from the toilets to another door. Part of him wanted to run like hell, but the detached, curious part overrode sense and lured him into following the footprints to a wider corridor with heavy doors on either side.

Prison cells, he thought with a shiver. As he stepped further into the corridor, he heard heavy breathing and the sounds of exertion.

"You know you want it, Dee," said a male voice.

Brendan guessed it came from a cell halfway down the hall with its door open. He cautiously stepped forward, staying out of sight. Once he was beside the door, he craned his neck around the doorframe.

Jaysus…

A pale, skinny ass attached to a pale, skinny dude bobbed up and down on the narrow bunk. Beneath him, a bound undead female trashed about. On the floor between the carnal scene and his vantage point lay two corpses, both with eye-wounds, one with a knife handle protruding from it. From what Brendan could make out, both were male and both still had their pants on, so the skinny dude hadn't fucked them like he was fucking the woman.

The man's tempo increased as he said, "I'm gonna cum, Dee. I'm gonna cum inside you."

Brendan couldn't help himself. "I don't think she gives a fuck, mate," he said.

The poor fucker was so shocked by the interruption he fell out of the undead woman and off the bunk right at the moment of orgasm.

Brendan almost felt sorry for him.

"What the hell?"

Brendan saw the fear of being discovered in the act, mixed with the pleasure of orgasm, mixed with something else. Disgust, maybe. Before Brendan could make another wisecrack at the dude's expense, his *object d'amour* tore herself free of her bindings and rose from the bed.

"What the hell?" said Eoin, shaking as he orgasmed and ejaculated from his fast-fading hard-on. He'd fallen awkwardly on his tailbone and gritted his teeth against the pain. All things combined made for a disorienting experience. *There you are.*

Standing outside the door stood a well-built guy with an amused expression. He held a hurley stick in one hand, but it was relaxed at his side. The guy's expression changed, his eyes widening as he looked at something behind Eoin.

Eoin turned in time to see what was once Deirdre lunge at him. He tried to move away, but the bodies of Mooney and Peter halted his progress.

Fucktard-Deirdre reached for him, teeth bared.

A *whoosh* as something swiped over him and cracked into Deirdre's skull. It knocked her sideways.

The guy from the door leaped across Eoin, following Deirdre as she fell.

Eoin turned on his side to watch, still gasping for breath.

The guy pummelled Deirdre mercilessly with the hurley stick.

"Stop!" Eoin cried, but the guy kept hitting her. "Please! Stop!" he shouted, as he reached out and grabbed the leg of the guy's jeans.

The guy came out of a violent haze. He breathed hard as he looked down at Eoin and, for a moment, Eoin thought the man would kill him. But he didn't. He sat back on the cell bunk, ignoring the blood and took in the room with a gesture of his arm. "Bet you have a story."

———

"And that's how I ended up in the cell... with Deirdre," said Eoin, before he inhaled deeply, finishing the joint.

Brendan had to admit, Eoin could handle his weed; he would have been toasted long ago, most likely hiding in a closet or jumping at his own shadow. Smoking wasn't Brendan's scene. He preferred being in control of his mental faculties.

"Do you think I'm going to hell?" asked Eoin.

"What's that?"

"Do you think I'll go to hell for doing that to Deirdre?"

Oh, here we go, thought Brendan. *The fucking drugs making him all philosophical.* He forced himself not to roll his eyes. "Nah. She was your girlfriend, right?"

"Yeah, but... she didn't give her consent... that's rape. I'm a rapist."

"Well, she was dead, mate," said Brendan in a serious tone that didn't reflect his interior mirth. "She was beyond giving consent."

"Fuck! That's worse. Fucking your dead girlfriend is fucked up!"

Brendan shook his head. "I think you're fine. She wasn't dead long. Think of her more as being recently alive. You made love to your recently alive girlfriend." He could see Eoin mull the concept over.

After a moment, Eoin nodded. "Recently alive. Yeah. That doesn't sound half as bad."

This dude needs to stop taking drugs, thought Brendan.

"But isn't it still necrophay... necropehell..." Eoin continued.

"Necrophilia? No way! She was moving, right? And still

warm? There's no way that counts as necrophilia. Guys who are into that want them cold and stiff."

Eoin breathed a sigh of relief. "Thank fuck for that," he said and got to work rolling another joint.

Brendan left him to it. "I'm going to check out the evidence room."

"Cool. Bring back any drugs you find, yeah?"

"Will do."

———

Brendan spent an hour ransacking the evidence room. He tipped the contents of each container on the table and put what he wanted into an empty box he'd placed on one side. Everything else, he swiped off the table with his arm to make room for the next container.

When he finished, he had a selection of recreational drugs, a dozen bladed weapons, an aged sawn-off shotgun with a box of shells, and a handful of gold jewellery. The latter was just in case anyone gave a shit about that sort of thing anymore.

He contemplated the contents of the box for a moment, then took out the harder drugs and pocketed them. *Don't want that cunt killing himself,* he thought. *Not yet, anyway.*

———

"Right. I'm off," said Brendan. He dropped the soft drugs he'd found in the evidence room, along with two of the poorer quality knives, on the seat beside Eoin.

"What?" asked Eoin, as he tried to work out what was going on.

"I'm heading off. That's the drugs I found, mostly weed, but some MDMA and amphetamine. And a couple of blades. Might come in handy." He packed the remaining items into the holdall he'd found in the station locker room and shouldered it. "Don't do anything I wouldn't do," he said in farewell and turned for the door.

"Wait!" Eoin jumped to his feet. He swayed a little but stayed upright. "Can I come with you?"

"What for?"

"For company?"

"Company?"

"Yeah, man. It's gonna get lonely with all the people gone and only fucktards around. We can keep each other company."

Brendan considered the stoner before him and weighed the pros and cons. In the end, he decided that another pair of eyes at his back might be worth the risk. And if Eoin became a liability, he could dispatch him with little effort. "Fine. I hope you know how to follow instructions."

Eoin gathered his things together and put them in his backpack. He gave the space a once-over and seemed satisfied he had everything, but then his eyes widened. "What about Deirdre?"

What the hell is he on about now? Brendan considered just ending Eoin there and then, but curiosity got the better of him. "You want to bring her with us?"

"No! But should we bury her?"

"You do what you need to do, man, but I'm going," said Brendan. Then he thought of the ransacked evidence room and the bodies in the cells. "Maybe burn the place?"

"Yeah. That's a great idea."

"I'll be outside." Brendan headed for the door.

"Thanks, Brendan. I'll be there in a minute. You won't regret it."

Brendan nodded. He doubted Eoin's abilities as an arsonist, but it would be an interesting test. *If he fucks it up, he's a dead man.*

———

Twenty minutes later, Eoin bolted from the front doors of the police station and ran to where Brendan stood beyond the barricades.

"How did you get on?" asked Brendan.

"Good. Yeah," said Eoin as he caught his breath. He'd been stacking furniture and documents in the rooms inside. He glanced at Brendan and sensed his expectation and knew the wisps of smoke curling from the station were underwhelming. "Wait for it," he said.

They stood looking at the station for a bit more. A seagull landed on the head of the guy he'd thrown off the rampart the night before. The bird plucked out one eyeball and swallowed it down while it was still attached to the dead guy. Eoin wondered what the guy's name was.

"Em. What are we—" Brendan began.

A massive explosion pushed the windows out in balls of flame.

Eoin turned away in time to protect his face, but he felt the heat on his side and the pressure in his ears. Tiny pieces of glass hit like bee stings.

When it subsided, an unearthly silence descended. Eoin thought he was deaf until Brendan spoke.

"What the fuck happened?"

Eoin straightened and brushed debris from his clothes. He picked glass shards from exposed areas of skin. "The gas. I turned it on and rigged a trigger." He wondered if Brendan was alright because he had a strange look on his face.

"You could have fucking warned me," said Brendan, after a while.

Eoin shrugged. "I didn't want to spoil the surprise." He looked back at the burning police station and felt an ache in his chest. *This is Deirdre's final resting place.* "Should I say a few words? Deirdre was the love of my life."

Brendan slapped him on the back and said, "There'll be plenty more Deirdres where we're going."

Eoin didn't quite know what Brendan meant, but he was glad of the sentiment. "I appreciate that, Brendan."

CHAPTER 14
K-HOLE

illian recognized the shift right away. Brendan was better at hiding it than Eoin, but not by much. Brendan's watchfulness turned full circle to where he avoided looking at her. Eoin grinned like a maniac whenever she caught his eye. *Why did I say anything about the child killer?* Sometimes she talked too much. There was an arrogance within her, she knew.

Lillian led the way up the steep hill to the town square, keeping enough distance between herself and the two men so there wouldn't be any surprises. She felt their eyes on her and considered turning and using the bow, but it would take too much time. The square ahead might be a better place.

The square was empty, of both the dead and the undead; she'd made sure of that. Resting her bag and bow on a bench, she took out her water bottle and took a swig. She used the movement as a distraction to release the catch on her belt knife. *Whatever is coming, I'll be ready*, she affirmed to herself.

When Eoin and Brendan approached, she offered them a drink. Both declined, but Brendan opened his pack and took out his own water bottle.

"What's the plan?" she asked.

Eoin looked nervous and was too quick to answer. "We've no plan."

Brendan was cooler. "Find a functioning car. Thought that was the plan for everyone."

"Yeah, sorry, I forgot," said Eoin, going so red it was almost cute.

What is their story? She wondered. They were such an odd pairing. Then she remembered their shared interest and her mood soured. *Just another pair of degenerates at the end of the world.*

———

Brendan took a long swig of his own water. His heart was racing, but he didn't show it. He closed the lid on the water bottle and stowed it in his pack. As quickly as he could, he took the hypodermic needle from where he'd placed it with his spare clothes. He stood, hiding the needle behind his leg. "Now!" he shouted.

Eoin, who was closer to Lillian, lunged forward and grabbed her in a bear-hug, trapping her arms at her sides.

Lillian reacted by freeing an arm and swiping at Eoin with her knife.

Eoin cried out in pain, but Brendan ignored it as he dashed around them. He darted in and plunged the needle into Lillian's left ass cheek, injecting the dose of ketamine.

Lillian wheeled around and slashed at him.

He jumped back, but not before taking a wound to the arm. He grunted in pain.

"Stay back or I'll kill you motherfuckers!" Lillian shouted. She crouched in a fighting stance with her left hand forward for blocking and her right hand in close to her body, ready to strike with the knife. Her eyes blazed with feral intensity.

"You won't be killing shit in a minute, bitch," Eoin said as he nursed the fresh wound on his shoulder.

"What did you give me?" She didn't look scared, she looked furious.

"Just a little Special-K," said Eoin, gloating.

"Shut the fuck up, Eoin," said Brendan. *Sometimes that cunt has a big mouth*, he thought.

"Fuck!" Lillian yelled, then turned and ran.

The move surprised Brendan, and he stood motionless for a moment before giving chase.

Eoin followed.

———

Eoin's shoulder hurt like a bitch. He gritted his teeth against the pain as he focused on Lillian's back. When they caught her, he'd make her pay.

Brendan was a short distance ahead of him, so he put his head down and caught up.

Brendan glanced at him as he drew alongside. "She has about twenty minutes, maybe less with the exertion," he said. "We just need to keep up."

Eoin nodded but thought, *Easier said than done.* He wasn't much of a runner and, as far as he was aware, neither was Brendan. He gave a silent prayer that Lillian was the same.

The fleeing woman kept to the right side of the street, close to the shopfronts. Then, suddenly, she dashed left and disappeared.

What the fuck!?

"Alley on the left," said Brendan.

As they got closer, Eoin saw it.

"Follow her. I'll cut around," said Brendan, and bolted back the way they'd come before Eoin could argue.

Eoin entered the alley and saw Lillian sprinting away, widening the gap between them. He raced after her, feeling the burn in his thighs. She disappeared over a slight rise and panic spurred him on. He was relieved to see her exit the alley, turning left as he crested the rise. *No, you don't!* When he exited the alley a moment later, she was nowhere to be seen. "Fuck!" He turned at the sound of running from his left.

Brendan came up the hill at a jog, face red as beetroot.

"Did you see her?" asked Eoin.

Brendan shook his head.

"She can't have gone far."

"Let's wait here."

———

Lillian lay behind the rusted railings of a red-bricked building. Running footsteps passed by her, followed by a "Fuck!" from Eoin. More footsteps came from the other direction, and Brendan's voice joined the conversation.

She fought to control her breathing and felt as though she might pass out, but she didn't dare allow herself to breathe hard. She groaned when Brendan suggested they wait. *I should have killed them,* she thought. But she hadn't acted when she'd had the opportunity, wanting to lead them somewhere she could take her time with them. She dismissed the thought. *No way to fix it now.*

Lillian didn't feel right at all but thought she was imagining it since Brendan only injected her a few minutes ago. *What the fuck will ketamine do?* She had never tried it, but recollected it being a horse sedative that some people took to have a good time. *Was it like LSD?* She'd never used that either but had seen plenty of references to it over the years.

"You'll probably start seeing things," said Gabe.

"Ssh. They'll hear you," she whispered. *Where did he come from?*

Gabe sat on the ground next to her, leaning his back against the wall. He smiled down at her, not bothered by the bloody slash wound in his neck. "Don't worry about them. They can't hear me anyway," said Gabe. As he spoke, the wound moved like a second mouth, blood bubbling out and running down his t-shirt.

"Why not?" she whispered, curiosity getting the better of her.

"Because I'm not here," he said. He reached across and tapped her temple. "I'm in your head."

As Gabe touched her, she felt her whole body become heavy. She tried moving her arms but didn't have the strength.

"Stay still, Lily. There's nowhere you need to be."

"Like hell there isn't," she said, anger flaring, but it extinguished just as quickly. "What happened to your neck?"

Gabe reached up and touched his open neck wound, sinking his fingers inside. "This? Don't you remember?"

"No." Blackness descended on her vision. "I don't remember."

The last thing she heard as the light left her world was Gabe saying, "This is from when you murdered me."

———

Eoin leaned against a rusted truck and lit a cigarette. He inhaled deeply and held it. "How long will it take?" he asked through an exhaled cloud of smoke.

"Another ten minutes." Brendan didn't know, but he wouldn't let Eoin in on that piece of information.

"Where did she go?" asked Eoin.

"She's here somewhere," said Brendan. That was the truth. *But where?*

Two churches stood in the vicinity, both with lots full of abandoned cars. A small Church of Ireland across from them and and the main Catholic one up the street on the right. When the world started to fall apart, the faithful descended upon their places of worship for guidance, or forgiveness, or whatever comfort it could offer.

"Maybe we should search the cars," said Eoin.

Brendan held up his hand in a silencing gesture. Had he heard something?

"What happened to your neck?" Lillian's voice, coming from behind them.

"Over there," said Eoin, quickly moving towards the red-bricked building at the mouth of the alley.

Brendan hurried after him.

They peered over the railing at the front of the building to see Lillian lying on the ground, eyes closed. "No," she murmured. "I don't remember."

"I wonder where she's gone," said Eoin.

"Nowhere around here," Brendan answered. "Come on, let's take her."

CHAPTER 15
DAY ZERO LILLIAN

Lillian soaked in a steaming hot bath as the sounds of "Gabriel" by Lamb played from the living room stereo. She'd turned the volume up loud enough to drown out the chaos of the streets.

She had been fond of the song even before Gabe claimed it in her thoughts. *Asshole!* she thought, but she didn't feel angry, just terribly sad. She thought Gabe was the one, her twin dark star; it always astonished her to have found him in the immense bleakness of her existence. Until the night before.

The streets had a carnivalesque atmosphere as Lillian navigated her way back home, with people spilling from packed clubs and bars onto the sidewalks. Everyone was desperate to enjoy themselves because, according to the news, they all lived on borrowed time. She didn't drink alcohol, having grown up in foster homes where that had been a real problem for her. She shivered at the memories and her thoughts turned to Gabe.

He worked the late shift tonight and wouldn't be home until morning. She hoped he'd be alright with the world going to shit around them. She smiled; Gabe could look after himself, of that she was certain. Still, if this was *The End*, she wanted to spend it with him. She hoped he would come home early.

She rounded a corner and tensed at the sight of the crowd

she'd have to pass through. A detour wasn't an option as it would add too much time to her journey, so she walked with a confident stride and put on an aggressive sneer to deter anyone who might get ideas about a lone female. She didn't have time to deal with that sort of thing. She put her hand in her coat pocket, gripped the screwdriver she always carried, and pushed her way in.

The crowd parted for her, and she made it to the other side without incident. As she passed the mouth of the next alley, she glanced in and did a double take.

Gabe reclined against the wall next to a beautiful young woman. He enchanted her with one of his angelic smiles as he leaned into her.

Lillian felt something vital, deep inside her, wither up and die as Gabe reached out and brushed a lock of hair away from the woman's face.

The woman smiled, all dimples and sunshine. In the next moment, her face contorted, her eyes lost focus, and her jaw slackened.

Confusion dawned on Gabe's face at the screwdriver which suddenly appeared in the woman's temple. He followed the arm, holding it to Lillian's enraged expression. "What the fuck, Lillian?"

Stabbing the woman in the head surprised Lillian as much as it surprised Gabe, but there was little to be done about it. "You told me you were working," she said as she pulled the screwdriver out.

The woman's body slid down the wall like a rag doll. A tiny stream of red flowed from the screwdriver hole down her cheek.

Lillian only had eyes for Gabe. She watched his internal struggle play across his face like a tempest.

"Fuck this," he said, coming to a decision. "I can't give you what you need." He turned and walked away.

Lillian followed, catching up to him. "All I need is you," she said, despising herself for being so pathetic. She reached for him, grabbed his arm, but he shrugged her off.

"You're unstable."

She felt panic well up inside her. She didn't want to lose him. "Stabilise me, please!"

Gabe pointed to the dead woman. "I didn't sign up for this."

Lillian's mood flipped to fury again as she rode a rollercoaster of pure emotion. "I never asked for your fucking signature!" she spat.

Gabe turned from her and hurried away, his expression disgusted and confused.

Lillian didn't follow; she returned to the dead woman and slid down the wall until she sat next to her.

"I don't blame you," she said to the dead woman as she rifled through her pockets. She found a pack of cigarettes and a disposable lighter. "I'm a health hazard." Lillian lit a cigarette and took a long drag. "If I was you, I'd leave me too," she said, thinking of Gabe as he walked away.

Her heart ached as she sat in the alley with the dead woman and remembered the night she first met Gabe.

———

Lillian stood on the street corner in the rundown part of town. She wore a short skirt and tight tank top with a pair of high leather boots, standard hooker issue. Her small teddy bear tattoo, with a scar over the heart which mirrored her own, was visible on her hip. She shivered against the freezing night and prayed for a John to come by soon.

As if in answer, a car turned her way. She struck a sensual pose as headlights illuminated the corner. The car crawled towards her, giving the driver plenty of time to check out the merchandise.

The window was down when it pulled in beside her and an almost handsome face peered out. Lillian moved closer, leaning down so her face was in view. The heat from the interior invited her in.

"How much?" asked the man.

"Depends on what you want," she said.

"A blowjob, for starters."

"Then it'll be eighty, for starters," she smiled and licked her lips to take any perceived sting from her words.

The man chuckled and said, "Hop in."

She walked around the front of the car so the guy could get another full look at her, then opened the passenger side door and got in.

"A gentleman would have opened my door," she teased.

"Get many gentlemen around here, do you?" he countered.

The man produced the cash from his wallet and handed it to her. This wasn't his first rodeo.

She took the money and spirited it away. "Drive straight on and take a right, it's private down there," she said.

"I know the spot."

Lillian rested her hand on the man's inner thigh, close to his crotch. *Poor bastard is already hard,* she thought as her little finger brushed the bulge in his pants.

He groaned and his breath quickened.

They turned down the side road and pulled in.

"Take it out," she commanded.

He obeyed.

She grabbed his hard member and crooned, "Lay back, close your eyes, and relax, baby."

He adjusted his seat back and relaxed into it with his eyes shut.

Lillian stroked his dick nice and slow to give her enough time to take her screwdriver out of its hiding place. Without a word, she plunged it to the hilt through the guy's closed left eye, deep into his skull. The other eye opened and he kicked the pedals, but Lillian stopped him with a twist of the screwdriver.

Lillian paused, dick in one hand and screwdriver in the other, and looked out the windows. Satisfied she had no unwanted observers, she got to work. First, she tucked the guy's dick back in his pants; it was no longer needed. Then, she used both hands to remove the screwdriver, cleaning off blood, brains, and eye jelly on the guy's shirt. Next, she reached across him and lowered his seat as far back as it would go, then got out of the car.

She slid into the back seat and produced a plastic bag and a zip-tie from her skimpy clothing. She was a regular magician. Covering the guy's head with the bag, she secured it around his neck with the zip-tie—she didn't want to have to explain the mess later. She dragged him across the lowered driver's seat into the back. It was a colossal effort since the guy was no lightweight, but she was stronger than she seemed.

Once he was in the back, she shut the door and got behind the wheel, adjusting the seat upright again. She started the car with the key that was still in the ignition and drove away from the cul-de-sac.

———

Lillian dragged the almost handsome guy's body from the back seat of his car onto the loose gravel of an empty carpark. The silhouettes of plant machinery rose into the air like mechanical beasts frozen in time.

She had scoped out the location over the preceding week and checked the place again just before looking for a victim earlier that evening. She knew precisely where to stash the body.

Lillian was elated; she would, once again, get away with disposing of another useless asshole. Since she fled from her hundredth foster home, she lived for ridding the world of useless, cheating, rapist, bastards. Preoccupied with her musings, she failed to observe the stranger until she collided with him. She whirled around at the touch to confront the person and saw her movements mirrored by a striking-looking man.

They both let go of what they carried and produced weapons, Lillian her screwdriver and this man, a claw hammer.

The man noticed Lillian's abandoned charge just as she noticed the lifeless female corpse he had been dragging.

She lowered her screwdriver and raised her eyebrow.

The man grinned boyishly at her as he lowered his claw hammer. "Hey," he said.

"Hey," she echoed.

"I'm Gabriel," he offered, tucking the hammer back into his belt and offering his hand.

Lillian hesitated for a second, then switched her screwdriver to her other hand and shook. "Lillian," she said.

"Don't suppose you could give a guy a hand?" he asked.

She looked around, half expecting a film crew to step out from behind a digger. When nothing like that happened, she shrugged. "Sure."

———

Lillian studied Gabriel out of the corner of her eye as the two of them worked to cover their respective victims. Both bodies lay at the bottom of what would become the foundations of an up-and-coming retail park.

Is this real?

Gabriel was, without a doubt, the handsomest man she had ever seen. *He either dropped from the heavens or spawned from hell,* she thought. Given the circumstances, she leaned towards the latter.

Gabriel threw a last shovel full of gravel onto the corpses and stood back to admire his work. He dazzled her with another smile.

She wished she wasn't so sweaty and dirty and dressed like a fucking skank.

"Do you want to get a drink?" he asked.

"What? Now?" she failed to keep the incredulity from her voice.

"No, I was thinking more tomorrow night," he said, brushing his hair back like some sort of model. "We can compare war stories," he added.

"Okay?" she was far from sure.

"Great!" He took the shovel from her; it was his after all. "I'll meet you on the square tomorrow night. Nine o'clock. Please don't stand me up." And with that, he was gone.

Fucking hell, she thought. She shivered, a reminder that the night was frosty and her fast-cooling perspiration wasn't helping. *What do I do about this guy?*

———

Lillian and Gabriel celebrated their six months anniversary with a romantic meal in a pleasant restaurant. Gabriel chose the venue and Lillian chose the couple for dessert. She still couldn't quite believe they'd found each other.

Partners in crime.

The Diabolic Duo.

They shared a bottle of wine as they watch the other patrons; a vigilant observer would note how little of their drinks they imbibed. An attractive couple walked by their table and left through the front door. Lillian and Gabriel follow them with hungry eyes.

They turned to each other and Gabriel raises an eyebrow.

Lillian subtly nodded, and the two stood and trailed the couple into the night.

On the street, their targets walked arm-in-arm to their car.

Lillian and Gabriel followed at a catch-up pace. As they closed in, they each drew their weapons. Perfectly synchronized, they murdered their victims. Lillian stabbed the man with her screwdriver, driving it from the base of his neck into his brain, while Gabriel hit the woman with his claw-hammer, caving in the back of her skull.

They carried the couple to their waiting car and sped away.

Later, beneath the leafy darkness of the woods, they dragged the pair through the underbrush. They turned to smile at each other every few paces. Lillian ached at how much she loved Gabriel, at how perfect her life was. They made love, passionately, beside the open grave, the dead couple bearing witness to their love.

Please let this last forever, thought Lillian, a silent prayer sent into the universe.

———

It didn't last for-fucking-ever, she thought.

The song "Apocalypse" by Cigarettes After Sex had taken over the stereo. Lillian closed her eyes and savoured it. *An appropriate song for the night*, she thought, with no trace of irony.

The bathwater was hot, but not uncomfortably so. She knew this would help the veins and arteries to stay open. The copious amount of water she'd drank earlier plumped her blood vessels, making them more visible, easier to find.

She reached out of the bath to the small side table and picked up the antique straight razor. It was purchased in a thrift store especially for the occasion. Lillian felt an affinity for it; both she and it being discarded things.

She held up the blade to examine it in the cold, fluorescent light, then swiped down experimentally. *It sings.* The hour she had spent sharpening it had paid off. *A box cutter would have served as well, but what would that say about me?*

Reflected light caught her eyes, and she slid deeper into the wet heat, allowing it to rise over her chin. The water lapped against her skin as two teary waterfalls flowed into it. She raised her left arm. Her right hand shook as she positioned the razor where she believed the radial artery to be. She pushed the tip of the blade into the flesh of her arm. A bead of blood welled up.

Lillian closed her eyes.

BANG, BANG, BANG, at the front door.

"Lillian!" called the distant voice of Gabriel.

Lillian's eyes sprang open.

BANG, BANG, BANG.

"Lillian! Open up!"

She rose from the bath and padded to the hallway, dripping water on the floor as she went. She held the straight razor loosely in her hand. She paused at the door and cocked her head to one side, listening.

"Trust" by The Cure played from the living room and sounds of distant screaming came from beyond the door.

THUMP, THUMP, THUMP on the door again.

"Lillian?" Gabriel was quieter.

Lillian opened the door.

Gabriel smiled his trademark boyish smile, a reminder of the night they met. There was a question in it.

She smiled back, tenderly, but her smile faded. She couldn't pretend. Not to Gabe. *This wound, I give myself.* She slashed the straight razor across Gabriel's throat.

With eyes widened in shock, he clutched his neck with both hands. Blood painted his fingers, and he emitted a gurgling sound, a suspended moment before he dropped to his knees.

Lillian didn't wait. She walked back along the hallway as Gabriel fell forward across the threshold and went still. Upon hearing him fall, the straight razor dropped from Lillian's hand, and she fell to her knees. Her shoulders shook as "Trust" ended and "Zombie" by The Cranberries began.

Unseen by Lillian, a tendril of darkness grew from a crack in the pavement and caressed Gabriel's foot where it touched the ground outside. It found bare skin at the top of his sock and disappeared into it like smoke in a breeze.

Lillian looked down at the blood splattered razor blade where it lay on the floor beside her. She reached down, picked it up again, and slowly gained her feet. She wasn't done with her fallen angel yet.

Gabriel's body lay face down with his legs half in, half out of the doorway.

Lillian rolled him onto his back and straddled his hips. She took her time cutting the buttons off his shirt, then she pulled it open to reveal the chest she'd spent many nights lying against, listening to the rhythm of his heart.

With steady, confident strokes, she carved the word 'FALLEN' across his chest as the world outside the doorway descended into chaos. She rose to survey her work, then leaned down to unbutton his pants. Reaching into his boxer shorts, she gripped the shaft of his penis and ball-sack in one hand and pulled them taut. She marvelled at how sharp the blade was as she cut his penis and ball-sack from his body with a single, practiced stroke.

As she stood again, Gabriel's penis in one hand and the straight razor in the other, she saw the first twitches of movement in his body. She'd anticipated it, after seeing news reports of it happening around the globe, but still, it amazed her.

I wonder if all the ones we killed together are returning like this, she pondered. She was uncertain whether she liked that idea; there was comfort to be had in the permanence of death.

Discarding his penis, she grabbed his legs and pulled him into the spare bedroom. As she locked him in there, she thought, *I'm not done with you just yet.*

CHAPTER 16
CHANGING LILLIAN

Brendan and Eoin stood in the function room doorway. Lillian lay on the floor in the middle of the room, lit by the beam of Brendan's torch. The rest of the room was in shadow; the sun had long since gone down.

They stripped Lillian naked and Brendan gazed appreciatively at her exposed body. It had been a long time since he'd seen a living woman in her full splendour. He paid particular attention to her scars, both self-inflicted and otherwise. For him, the blemishes had a way of accenting the beauty.

The hard fold of skin beneath her left breast was an old knife wound; he'd bet his life on it. *There's a story there*, he thought. He noticed the cute teddy bear tattoo on her hip had stitches in the same place, which he thought was interesting. He almost regretted what they were about to do to her because he'd never know the answers to his questions, but he was certain Lillian was too dangerous to keep alive.

"She'll be the hottest one yet," said Eoin. He looked at Lillian with hunger in his eyes.

"She will," Brendan agreed. "Bring him in."

Eoin hastened down the corridor and out of sight, only to reappear a moment later with a zombie held in an animal catcher. They'd taken him from the row of the castrated fucktards leading into town. The word *'FALLEN'* was carved across his chest.

Lillian groaned at that moment and the fallen zombie snapped his head up, attentive.

"Release him," said Brendan.

Eoin released the fallen zombie from the snare and retreated to the doorway.

It stood like a statue in the centre of the room.

Lillian shifted position and groaned again.

The undead man zeroed in on her with his zombie-radar and shuffled towards her.

"He's a slow cunt, isn't he?" said Eoin.

"He's old. One of her first," said Brendan. He closed the door, blocking Lillian and the zombie from view. "Stay here until it's done. Make sure she doesn't get out."

"Where are you going?"

"To fix up a cocktail for the party," Brendan said with a smile.

"Oh, yeah. Great," said Eoin, sounding less than enthusiastic.

What the fuck is up with him now? wondered Brendan. He clapped Eoin on the shoulder and said, "Think about all the fun we'll have afterwards. Don't fuck this up."

———

Lillian surfaced from blackness to shadows. She groaned and one shadow broke away, becoming a lurching figure above her. She still transitioned from dream to wakefulness. "Gabriel?"

As the shambling figure closed on her, she caught the musty scent of decay. Discoloured teeth appeared, snarling from the gloom. The figure lurched, snapping those teeth at her face.

She scrambled to one side and pushed him, but he fell on top of her. She moved her hands in front of her in time to stop the second bite. "Fuck!" she cried, trying to recall where she was and how she got there. Her last clear memory was running from Eoin and Brendan and seeing Gabriel. *But Gabe is long dead,* she thought.

The creature on her possessed a wiry strength and she struggled against him. She was conscious of his decayed flesh touching her skin. If she wasn't fighting for her life, she might have shivered to death.

He lunged again and part of his shoulder crumbled beneath her hand. He snapped his head forward, and she had no choice but to push his head away with her other hand.

She felt the sharp pain in the flesh of her palm before she realized he'd bitten her. She screamed then, knowing it was a death sentence. With the infusion of adrenaline, she threw him off her and got to her feet. "Fuck! Fuck! Fuck!"

The door opened and she squinted at the light shining upon her. The light moved to Gabriel. Poor, pathetic, dead Gabriel. Having the last fucking laugh after all this time.

He stood up again and Lillian prepared to pre-emptively defend herself, despite the sharp pain in her hand which announced her doom. She had never been one to back away from a fight, and she wasn't about to start. "To the last fucking breath, motherfucker," she said, unsure if she spoke to undead Gabriel, the torch-man, or both.

Torch-man moved into the room, and she readied herself.

———

"Don't fuck this up," said Eoin, mimicking Brendan's voice once he was well out of earshot. *Who the fuck does he think he is bossing me around?* If Eoin wanted a mother, he would have dug up his own long ago. "Fucking prick," he muttered, not prepared to shout it, just in case. He heard a noise coming from the other side of the door. Was Lillian conscious?

"Fuck!" she said, clear and loud.

Curious, Eoin bent an ear to the door. He heard sounds of a struggle. Someone falling? Then a scream of pain and more sounds of violence.

"Fuck! Fuck! Fuck!" from Lillian, a lot more distressed.

Eoin didn't know what he should do. He tried to think what Brendan would want him to do. *What if she's being eaten?* He was sure Brendan wouldn't want that, so he pushed open the door and shone in his torch.

Lillian cowered naked in its beam, clutching her left hand.

He could see teeth-marks. *Fuck! She's bitten!* He turned the beam on the fucktard and saw it regain its feet and turn toward her again. *Oh, no you don't!* He rushed in, drawing his machete and met the fucktard with a powerful overarm swing. The blade made a satisfying *thunk* as it penetrated the top of the skull.

The fucktard dropped where he stood.

Eoin pulled the blade free and turned to face Lillian.

Tears streamed down her face, but there was fight in her.

He thought back to Red Jacket and the last night he partied with Brendan. He took no pleasure from the memory, just a feeling of disgust mixed with regret. Did he want to watch Lillian turn so they could fuck her while out of their minds? He couldn't speak for Brendan, but Eoin didn't want to do that shit anymore. He could only imagine the trouble he'd be in with Brendan if he messed up his grand plan, though.

Fuck Brendan, he thought. He'd help Lillian in the only way left to help her.

———

Lillian squinted into the torch beam, prepared to fight this motherfucker tooth and nail if he got close. *Eoin*. She wondered if she'd infect him if she sank her teeth into his flesh but dismissed the idea. *Too fucking soon*, she thought. She might do it anyway, just for spite. Brendan might kill him if he thought he was infected.

Thoughts of the bite made her look around the room for something to tie off her arm. She couldn't see anything and the bastards had stripped her of clothing, so she had nothing to rip a tourniquet from. Eoin was dressed though…

"Let me help you," said Eoin in a hushed voice.

"How will you do that?" she asked.

"You're bitten."

"Fuck you, Eoin," she spat.

The torch beam shone wildly about the room as Eoin sheathed the machete and raised his hands.

"I'll make it quick," he said.

Is this prick being compassionate? Lillian thought he was. She considered her options for a moment before nodding.

"Okay," she said. "Can you make it clean? To the neck?"

"I'll try," he said.

Lillian didn't press the matter; there were no other volunteers. "What do you need me to do?" she asked.

Eoin placed the torch on the ground so that the beam fell on Lillian. "Just lie there and stay still."

She lay in the beam of light with her right ear to the ground. She watched Eoin unsheathe the machete and hold it in a two-handed grip.

He swung down in practice, then turned to her. "Look, I'm really sorry," he said.

"Save it," she interrupted. "Just fucking do it."

He nodded and raised the machete over his head. He cried out as he brought the blade down like a discount store samurai.

At the last moment, Lillian moved her head back and brought her left hand up to where her neck had been. Eoin had no time to correct the strike. The blade cut into Lillian's arm just below the wrist, nearly severing her hand.

Fiery agony seared through Lillian's body, threatening to make her pass out. She fought against it as she lurched to her feet, her mostly severed hand flopping uselessly as it hung from her arm by a small section of skin and muscle. Blood spurted from the exposed blood vessels onto the torch lens, painting the room crimson.

Eoin was knocked off balance, but recovered. As he moved in for a second strike, Lillian shoved her stump in this face. Blood spurted out and struck him in the eyes. He cried out in rage and confusion and dropped one hand from the machete to wipe away the blood.

Lillian used the opportunity to rush in and kick his kneecap. A crack sounded as Eoin's kneecap shattered and his leg bent in the wrong direction.

Eoin screamed and dropped the machete as both hands sought his injured knee.

Lillian rushed to pick up the blade and, wielding it one-handed, swung it at Eoin. The blade cut deep into the exposed side of his neck, and he fell to the floor. She stepped back, prepared to deliver another blow, but Eoin only looked at her, surprised and hurt, as the blood pumped from the deep wound to his neck.

He tried to say something, but all that came out was a bloody gargle, followed by scarlet bubbles. The flow of blood from Eoin's neck tapered off and Lillian watched as the life left his eyes.

Using the machete, she gritted her teeth and chopped her hand free. Fresh agony lanced through her. Shaking it off, she ripped a section from Eoin's shirt and looped it around her upper arm, using her hand and teeth to tie the ends together. Then, using the machete handle as a windlass, she twisted the improvised tourniquet to apply pressure. It was cumbersome but, before long, the bleeding was under control. A wave of dizziness washed over her and she sent out a silent prayer that she wouldn't pass out.

The long blade was easy to keep in position, but it was her only weapon. She searched Eoin's body, but he had no backup. He had pants and boots, which she relieved him of, no simple task in her condition. The sizes were wrong, but better than being naked.

She used what remained of Eoin's shirt to cover her bloody stump. Picking up the torch, she left the room. Finding a safe place to properly tend to her wound before she passed out was her priority. *If I don't turn,* she thought. That was still a possibility; she may not have amputated her hand in time. She hoped she would live to find out; she had unfinished business with Brendan.

———

Brendan stood in the doorway, staring at Eoin's dead body, bloody and naked except for socks and a pair of stained boxer shorts. "For fuck's sake!"

It was the saddest thing Brendan had ever seen. He couldn't believe his friend's life had ended like this; Eoin deserved more.

The fallen undead was there too, lying on the floor with a cracked open skull.

Something else lay close to Eoin in a pool of blood. *Is that a hand?* Brendan moved closer. *It is a fucking hand!*

Brendan saw the bite-mark on the palm and wondered what went down. He might never know unless he found Lillian. How far could she have gotten with such an injury?

Not far, he thought.

He loaded the hypodermic needle with a fresh dose of ketamine. He had just the thing for her when he caught up.

CHAPTER 17
TRAUMA SURGERY

illian panicked when she awoke in the disorienting darkness. Her body ached in the cramped surroundings. For a moment, she thought Eoin and Brendan still held her captive, but then she remembered being bitten and tricking Eoin into amputating her hand.

Her stump throbbed when she thought of the incident, inciting a fresh wave of pain. She would need to take more pain killers, but other than that, she felt okay. The fact she maintained her ability to think and reason indicated she caught the infection in time.

Lillian reached over her head and found the edge of the morgue drawer frame. With some effort, she got the bed moving and slid it out. She was in the county morgue preparation room. The medical supplies she used to tend to her wound the night before lay upon the stainless-steel embalming table.

She swung her legs off the drawer bed and stood, experiencing a wave of light-headedness. She hadn't eaten since the previous morning but she would have to worry about that later.

She padded across the cold tiles to the embalming table and shook pills from the two bottles she'd left there the previous evening. One contained codeine, to stave off the approaching pain; the other was a strong antibiotic to fight infection in her arm. She swallowed two pills from each with a mouthful of water.

Her memory of the night before was a series of flashed

images, punctuated by pain. She'd come close to passing out but fought through it to clean and dress her wound. After taking the first dose of pills, she climbed into the morgue drawer. Blessed oblivion took her as the drawer slid closed.

As she considered her next move, she prepared an injection, then stored the unused supplies and binned the waste materials. The machete she cleaned and kept close by.

A sound, out of place, at the edge of hearing, made her pause. *What was that?* She froze in place, concentrating on the noises around her as she tried to catch any sound which didn't belong.

There! A small stone skittered across a footpath outside.

She took the needle and placed it between her teeth before grabbing the machete and padding back to the morgue drawer and closing herself inside.

———

As Brendan followed the blood droplets, he crept closer to the mortuary. He'd lost the trail in the dark of the previous night, but at first light, he'd ventured out and picked it up again. He moved carefully, trying to avoid any more stones.

The mortuary's front entrance was open a hand's breadth. He paused there to listen. Only silence from inside, so he eased the door open enough to pass through. Morning light streamed through the window, illuminating the small reception area. The trail of blood led from where he entered to a door marked 'Private'.

As stealthily as possible, Brendan crossed to the private door. He adjusted his grip on his large hunting knife before pushing down on the handle. The mechanism squealed in protest as the door opened, and he flinched at the sound.

The trail of blood continued across the tiled floor of the private room to a metal table at its centre. The table was so clean it gleamed, sign enough for Brendan of recent use. He entered the room for a closer look.

To his left were three rows of four morgue drawers, all closed. He'd inspect those in a moment, but the far end of the room drew his attention. He crossed to stand before the shelves packed with specimen jars. It took him some time to realize what he was looking at, like an optical illusion where you see the lady but not the crone until—

Holy fucking Jesus!

Each specimen jar contained a severed penis and an accompanying set of balls. Brendan's eyes watered at the sight of the collection. A quick count gave him close to a hundred jars. He cast his mind back to the walk into town and came up with a similar number. *One jar for each of those poor cunts*, he thought.

He felt a sting in his neck and swatted it away.

"What the hell?" he exclaimed. He looked at his hand and saw a smear of blood.

Lillian stood behind him, pale as fuck but smiling pleasantly, holding an empty syringe. "Night, night," she said, from what sounded like very far away.

Then, the lights went out.

———

Lillian went to work as soon as Brendan hit the floor. She employed the mortuary's body lift to move him from the floor onto the embalming table. Once there, she stripped him and shaved the chest and groin areas, then disinfected both.

Another wave of light-headedness hit her, so she paused long enough to eat two meal replacement bars and wash them down with a bottle of water. She felt much better after getting food into her belly and started back with renewed energy.

The procedure took much longer than usual, one-handed and tired as she was, but she made steady progress through the day. She wondered if there were any one-handed surgeons in the world. The scalpel work was fine, but cauterizing and suturing blood vessels and keeping the area free of blood were challenging.

She stood back hours later, wiping sweat from her brow with a bloody sleeve. *Not my finest work*, she admitted. *But not bad, all things considered.*

In the fading daylight, Lillian hurried to clean and bandage Brendan while she could still see. She lifted his penis and balls from where they lay on the stainless-steel table and transferred them to the waiting specimen jar. With great care, she placed the jar where Brendan would be sure to see it upon waking.

Before leaving, she administered another shot to keep him out until morning.

———

Brendan woke feeling groggy, but kept his eyes shut and his breathing steady. He sensed the coolness of metal beneath him and remembered the mortuary bench. That memory triggered one of an insect sting, followed by Lillian holding up a needle.

Shit…

Warm daylight shone on his face but he couldn't tell how much time had passed since she drugged him. Maintaining his steady breathing, he strained to listen for signs of Lillian's presence.

Nothing.

He noticed a peculiar tightness around his groin and across his chest and panic hit him. All thoughts of subterfuge fled. He opened his eyes as his hands went down. "Fuck!" he cried at the absence which greeted him.

He scoured the room. His eyes stopped at the specimen jar at the foot of his makeshift bed. Floating there, suspended in fluid, were what he assumed were his testicles and penis. He stared at them, mesmerized, wondering how he felt. *How should I feel?*

They looked sort of pathetic floating in the specimen jar; he didn't know whether he should laugh or cry.

The door opened, and Lillian entered carrying a tray.

"What the fuck did you do to me?" Brendan demanded.

"Do I need to draw you a diagram?" she enquired.

He experienced a brief flash of the castrated undead leading into town. He gritted his teeth. "You're not putting me out there," he said.

"You all end up out there. But not today." She crossed to where he lay and placed the tray next to him.

His stomach rumbled as the scent of fresh soup wafted to him.

"Today is for rest and recovery," she said as she crossed back to the door. Then, she was gone.

Brendan's stomach growled again, and he realized he was ravenous. *Fuck it,* he thought. *I'm not dead yet.* He lifted the bowl of soup and took a deep drink, feeling the stretch in his chest. His torso was covered in a blood-soaked bandage. A detached part of him wondered what moniker she'd given him. He smiled grimly. *So many to choose from.*

Lillian closed the preparation room door behind her and stumbled across the reception area to lean against the desk for support. Her vision swam and her hands shook; she was exhausted. It had taken more strength than she could spare to keep herself together in front of her patient.

She knew she should have rested after performing Brendan's operation, but she needed to check the surrounding area for interlopers, both living and otherwise. All was clear apart from a couple of wandering dead, which she promptly dispatched to whatever hell they went. But it had taken time, and she had only enough left to prepare food before Brendan was due to wake.

She had almost added a lethal dose of poison to the soup before thinking better of it. It was a mystery to her as to why she held back. There was something about the man Lillian couldn't figure out. That alone should have been enough reason to dispose of him promptly.

Get some sleep, she ordered herself. She was sure things would be clearer after she rested. She would, likely, have Brendan tied to a lamppost before the week was out.

CHAPTER 18
RECUPERATION

Brendan stood before the mirror and stroked the weeks growth of beard on his face appreciatively.

I could get used to this, he thought as he scratched his cheek furiously, *if I can ignore the damned itching.*

The wound in his groin itched too but he dared not touch it yet.

Lillian changed the bandages daily and inserted a new catheter each time.

He hadn't been tempted to look. It was time to look at his chest though. It was the reason for being before the mirror.

Lillian tended to that wound too, but kept him from seeing what was carved there. "I wouldn't want to ruin the surprise," she said.

Well, fuck surprises. He waited until she was gone before he made his way to the only mirror in the building. He peeled back the surgical tape from the top left corner, just over his heart, and pulled the bandage away. The engraved flesh had begun to heal but the cuts were deep and had plenty of healing left. There were black stitches placed regularly; he supposed he ought to be grateful to Lillian for that much.

The first three letters above his left nipple read *'ETA'*, in all-caps, like he was shouting. *Estimated Time of Arrival, motherfuckers,* he thought. He gritted his teeth and pulled the dressing off completely, ripping out some newly sprouted stubble from the edges. The rest of the letters said *'RENEGED'. What does that mean?* He wondered what renouncing an ETA could refer to. Was there a deeper meaning to be had from the phrase? His puzzled expression morphed into realization, and he chuckled. *You fucking eejit,* he thought. He was looking at the word in the mirror.

The word carved into his chest was *'DEGENERATE'.*

His chuckle faded, replaced by a rueful smile. He had to admit, degenerate was an apt description for him. At least for the man he used to be. He wasn't so sure anymore.

For as long as he could remember, there were two sides to him. Not personalities, more like distinct modes of operation. One side was cold and calculating, guided by a razor-sharp analytical mind. Solid, logical, and ruthless. The other side was twisted and perverted, guided by sexual impulses and obsessions, always striving for the next carnal experience. That latter side had the ability to cloud, and often override, the analytical side, much to the dismay of his logical self, usually in hindsight. He'd grown accustomed to it, though, and an uneasy alliance formed over the years.

Circumstances had rendered that alliance obsolete. The physical driver of that wayward part of himself had been removed and he was adjusting to a new reality, a reality where, arguably, the more dangerous part of himself had full control.

He placed the dressing back over the reminder of his former self, careful to line up the tape with the marks on his skin. Then, he shuffled back to bed.

———

Lillian wedged the tip of the crowbar between the doorframe and the edge of the church's heavy, iron-banded door. She worked it in until she was sure she'd penetrated deep enough, then pushed with all the strength she could muster. The wood cracked and splintered, and the door opened with an exhalation of dust.

Reluctant to breathe in the expelled air, she pulled a bandanna from her pack and tied it around her neck using her hand and teeth, then pulled it up to cover her mouth. It wasn't the best mask in the world, but it would offer some protection. She made a mental note to locate more effective masks for her next trip.

With the bandanna secured, Lillian took a flashlight from the pack before entering the gloomy interior. She crossed the compact antechamber immediately inside the doorway which led to the nave of the church where the congregation sat.

"Jesu—" she began, then bit off the casual use of the Lord's name.

From the back of the nave to the altar at the front sat row upon row of the dead. Lillian stood statue-still but no sound or movement came from them. Couples embraced or simply held hands. Families crowded together seeking solace. Individuals knelt with heads bowed and hands clasped.

What happened here? She walked along the aisle towards the front and saw the same patterns of solace and supplication repeated. There were no signs of violence, nothing to indicate how these people met their end. None of them looked as though they had turned into the shambling creatures she had become so used to dealing with.

When Lillian reached the end of the aisle, she saw a figure hunched over before the altar. She approached the figure cautiously, wishing she had Gabriel or Brendan to watch her back and take the edge off the uneasiness she felt.

She frowned, not quite sure why she'd want her patient by her side for this, nor why he would occur in the same thought as her dead lover.

On closer inspection, she noticed the figure wore the vestments of a Catholic priest. His pose struck her as unusual in that he knelt with his back to the altar, facing the congregation rather than looking up at Christ hanging on his cross. A look of serenity was evident upon the priest's face.

Lillian shoved the unnervingly upright priest with her boot and he toppled over, raising a cloud of dust. He remained unmoving, as did the silent congregation.

A shiver touched her lower spine and trembled its way up her back. She had no way of knowing what went on in the church, nor why none of the amassed congregation turned into undead abominations, but she knew, instinctively, she didn't belong in this place; it felt like something was pushing her away.

I wonder what Brendan would make of this. Another frown. *What does it matter what he makes of anything?*

In that moment, she decided when Brendan was strong enough, she would bring him to the church to garner his opinion on the dead congregation, but only on their way to the far side of town.

———

Another week and Brendan stood before the mirror once more. His beard was thicker, and the word wound had mended nicely, though not completely. He felt he passed a precipice, both mentally and physically. His strength returned for the latter while the former sought new heights, unshackled by urges which had been ever-present before his operation. *A blessing or a curse?* He couldn't definitively decide.

For large swathes of time during the days of his recuperation, he felt like he'd been cleansed, and his physical sacrifice represented a chance at a new life. The possibilities excited him. At other times, a malicious voice in his head called for revenge on Lillian for what she'd done.

Over the preceding two weeks, he was surprised to find that he didn't miss his manhood at all. Acclimating to pissing sitting down took some time, but it was much tidier. And the clarity that came with the absence of his more unusual urges was transcending.

Lillian had been the perfect host, nursing him back to health and seeing to his needs.

For his part, he'd been the accepting patient. He had little choice, but he'd be lying if he denied he assumed his role easily.

Brendan reached down the front of the bottoms he wore and retrieved the knife he'd secreted there. He'd taken the knife from a tray of food a week ago and it had, apparently, gone unnoticed. The blade was dull, but he'd sharpened it using the base of a coffee mug.

He didn't know what he would do with the blade, but he felt better having it.

Hearing the exterior door open, he put the knife away mere moments before Lillian arrived.

She stood in the doorway with an unreadable expression and the animal catcher held in her only hand. "It's time," she said.

Brendan looked at the animal catcher and raised a questioning eyebrow. "Is that necessary?"

"Is it a problem?"

Brendan shrugged and walked to the door. Animal catcher or not, this ends today. One way or another.

CHAPTER 19
ALLEGIANCE

illian walked into town, Brendan leading the way.

He was shirtless, the word *'DEGENERATE'* declared in angry scabs across his chest for all the world to see. The wound mended nicely over the past two weeks, which was more time than she'd given to any of her other projects.

She gripped the handle of the animal catcher tightly, the other end looped loosely around Brendan's neck. He wouldn't try to escape, she was sure of that, having come to know the man in the time since his operation. *If he makes a move it'll be when I'm distracted; not like this.*

She felt a peculiar sensation, and it surprised her to realize it was regret gnawing at her stomach. Not regret at anything she'd done to him, regret over what there was still to do. *I'll get over it. I always do.*

They were on the way to the church in the centre of town. She really wanted to know his thoughts on the dead congregation.

She looked down at the stump, covered in an improvised leather cap. It healed well, and she had almost stopped reaching for things with it and being surprised that it wasn't there. All part of the process, she supposed.

They approached a junction, the last before the church, and she pulled back on the animal catcher to halt Brendan.

He stopped obediently. "It looks clear," he said, somehow reading her mind. And he was correct. It *looked* perfectly clear.

"Uh huh," she said. *So why do I think something's wrong?*

———

Brendan stood in the middle of the street, taking it all in. The warmth of the sun on his back, the wind across his healing chest, birds in the sky, all that shit. It was good to be outside and good to be alive. *For however long it'll last.* He turned to look at Lillian. "Should we go on?" he asked.

She scanned the ground before them, lips tightened to a line, then nodded.

Brendan continued past the traffic light sentinels. Before they crossed the junction, he heard a *whoosh* followed by the *thump* of impact. He waited for the accompanying pain, but none came. Behind him, Lillian crashed to the ground.

"Woo-hoo, got her!" came a cry from his left.

"Nice one!" another called from the right.

Brendan remained impassive as the assailants stepped in from either side, a young woman from the right, and a young man from the left. Another man, older than the two, stood from his place of concealment further up the street and approached.

Lillian groaned.

The woman strode by Brendan, full of youthful cockiness. She made a beeline for Lillian. "It's the fuckin' bitch that killed Anto, alright," she said and savagely kicked Lillian's stomach, then hawked and spat on her face.

The young man approached more slowly and lingered on Brendan. "Would ya look at the state a' this poor cunt?" he said. He bent close and moved his lips as he read the word on Brendan's chest. "Jaysus! Look what's writ on him! He's a fuckin' degenerate!" Evidently, the young man was much amused.

The older man reached the group and paused before Brendan to gently remove the loop from around his neck. "There ya go, bud," he said in a compassionate voice. "Yer safe now." The man shot the young guy a warning look, which had an intimidating effect. Then, the man focused on the young woman laying into Lillian. "Calm down, Brid," he said. His tone worked to rein her in. He walked to Lillian and hunkered down.

———

Lillian tried to focus on the man squatting in front of her. Her head spun from whatever had knocked her from her feet, and she was sure the young bitch had broken a rib or two.

"You shouldn't have killed the lads, miss," the man said, very reasonably.

She spat blood from a bitten tongue onto his boots in reply.

He responded by taking a fistful of her hair in a vice-like grip. He stood, and she had no choice but to follow. A vicious gut punch knocked the wind out of her.

Brid danced about chanting, "Kill the bitch! Kill the bitch!"

Lillian pulled a ragged breath into her lungs as the man dragged her to the middle of the junction.

"Oh, the bitch is dead, Brid," he said as he kicked the back of Lillian's legs to bring her to her knees. "But this poor cunt has as much right to killing her as us."

Lillian studied Brendan's face, but it was impassive.

"Hold her," the man commanded.

The youths each took an arm and pulled back on them.

Lillian gritted her teeth against the pain in her shoulders but refused to cry out; not for the likes of these.

The man unsheathed a knife and handed it to Brendan hilt first. "Here you go, brother." He steered Brendan to Lillian with a guiding hand on his shoulder.

Lillian looked into Brendan's emotionless eyes, thinking, *Is this it?*

Behind Brendan, the man drew a revolver from his belt.

———

The knife felt good in Brendan's hand. The solidity of it spoke of quality construction, no knock-off Rambo knife, but a tool for getting work done. Much better than the blade he had hidden down his pants.

Lillian knelt before him, arms stretched out behind her by the head man's minions. Even meeting her end like this, there wasn't an inch of give in her. She looked Brendan straight in the eye, then flicked a look behind him.

He grasped her meaning instantly. *This prick is up to something.* Brendan flipped the knife to a back-hand grip, as he turned his towards the man. "Hey."

The man looked up, guiltily.

Brendan was already moving. He ducked and pivoted right, swinging his knife-wielding right hand behind him.

A shot fired wild above Brendan a moment before he sunk the knife to the hilt in the man's stomach. The man howled in agony.

Brendan turned to face the man and said, "I'm not your fucking brother," before he twisted the knife and pulled it sideways across the man's belly.

The man's howl turned to screams of agony as his insides flopped onto the ground.

Brendan dropped the knife and picked up the revolver. He turned to the young sidekicks. "Run."

The two remained motionless.

Brendan closed the gap between them in two strides and shot the boy in the head at point-blank range. The round must have been modified, because half of the lad's head disintegrated, gore decorating the girl's face and clothing.

Brendan turned to her. "I said *run!*"

She did.

As she sprinted away, he counted under his breath, "One, two, three," he raised the gun and sighted on her, "four, five, six, sev—"

Lillian's hand touched the top of the revolver and pushed it down. "Leave her," she said.

He raised an eyebrow but didn't protest. He shrugged and said, "As you wish."

The man's screams echoed behind them as he futilely attempted to place his intestines back into his stomach. They slipped through his fingers, but he refused to give up, desperation plain on his face.

The noise drilled into Brendan's brain, causing him to wince. "What about him?" he asked.

Lillian was already on it. She picked up the knife Brendan used to open the guy's stomach. A solid kick to the chest knocked the man to his back, where Lillian mounted him. She went to work on the man's upper torso and head, stabbing him in a calculated manner as she kept him in place with her leather-clad stump.

Brendan didn't know how long it took, but when she'd finished with him, the man was pulped, bloody, and silent, his skull stripped naked.

Lillian, painted scarlet, breathed hard.

A tool for getting work done, thought Brendan. He walked to her and offered his hand. She accepted his help, and he bore her weight as she stood.

"There'll be more of them," he said.

She nodded as she surveyed the carnage. "We'll be alright," she said.

Brendan almost didn't register it, but his stomach gave a slight lurch upon replaying her last sentence. "We?" he asked.

"Have something better to do?"

Her question teased him, he knew. "Well, now that you mention it…" he said.

Lillian smiled, her teeth dazzlingly bright in contrast to her bloody face. "Come on, I have something to show you," she said, and took off up the street towards the church.

He fell in step behind her, excited by what the future might bring.

CHAPTER 20
SHADOW

The undead child hung from the bridge on meat-hooks, one among many. She was twelve, or had been when she turned. She had no concept of where she was, where she'd been, or whom.

A tendril of shadow moved into her and the infinitesimal residue of consciousness that remained retreated from the cold. The Shadow permeated her body, expanding until it overflowed. The Shadow tested its new host and found it restricted. With boundless patience, it worked to free its limbs. Once unfettered, it hung only from the hook attached to its neck, swaying in the breeze. With both hands, it reached up and located the chain above. It pulled steadily upward and detached itself, then let go. Dropping to the hard road, it stumbled but corrected itself. It stood straight and surveyed its surroundings.

Stray souls lined the road ahead, their husks tethered on either side. The Shadow had much work to do.

THANK YOU

Thank you for reading Shadow Apocalypse. If you enjoyed this book please consider leaving an honest review on Amazon.

Red Jacket, a short prequel to Shadow Apocalypse, is available to subscribers of my newsletter at bchollywood.com/newsletter

RED JACKET: A PREQUEL TO SHADOW APOCALYPSE

THE DARKLE CHRONICLES
BOOK TWO

ACKNOWLEDGMENTS

I would like to extend my gratitude to the following individuals for their invaluable support and contributions to this project:

My family, for their unwavering love and encouragement throughout my writing journey. Your belief in me sustained my spirits.

My editor, Mary, whose keen insights, meticulous editing helped shape this manuscript into its final form.

My beta readers, Shannon, Heather, and Derek, who provided feedback and helped me refine the narrative. Your insights were invaluable.

The guys at the Written in Red podcast, Aron, Carver, Daniel, and Rowland, for reigniting the flame.

The readers, for taking this journey with me. Your interest in my work is the greatest reward.

This book would not exist without your collective contributions, and I am deeply grateful for every one of you.

With sincere appreciation,
B.C. Hollywood
October, 2023

ABOUT THE AUTHOR

B. C. Hollywood is an Irish author of dark fiction and extreme horror. He spends much of his spare time battering raw story ideas into shapelier form.

He writes novels, short stories, flash fiction, screenplays, and poetry. He is the author of *Dogcatcher: A Short Story*, the collection *Add me… and other warnings,* and the extreme horror series, **The Darkle Chronicles,** of which *Shadow Apocalypse* is book one.

To connect with B.C. and for news of his upcoming titles, check out his website www.bchollywood.com and subscribe to his newsletter.

The second book in **The Darkle Chronicles** series, *Once Upon a Time in Monto,* is out now and the third book, *The House of Marionettes,* releases Summer 2024.

* 9 7 8 1 0 6 8 6 7 5 7 1 3 *